Meet Hetta Moon

Meet

Hetta Moon

Carol Frey Yingling

MEET HETTA MOON

ISBN 978-0-9895914-2-3

For Lore Frey, who proves adventure knows no age limits

and with thanks and my unending gratitude to Anna D, who read and advised, Christine, who both advised and encouraged (sometimes with coffee, sometimes with threats), and Mary Yingling, for her continuing encouragement and support

Table of Contents

Chapter 1: MY WORLD CHANGES...1

Chapter 2: FOR THE WORSE...3

Chapter 3: PIECES TO PICK UP 6

Chapter 4: DROPPING SOME PIECES 10

Chapter 5: ICE CREAM THERAPY WORKS...13

Chapter 6: DEREK IRONS...22

Chapter 7: A POSSIBILITY...26

Chapter 8: I WAIT..32

Chapter 9: SELECTED AS A GAL FRIDAY 37

Chapter 10: I BECOME INDISPENSABLE...40

Chapter 11: THINGS FALL INTO PLACE...45

Chapter 12: IT'S ALL FUN AND GAMES….......................................47

Chapter 13: …UNTIL SOMEONE GETS HURT.......................................50

Chapter 14: I ATTEMPT TO SLEUTH 57

Chapter 15: MY SLEUTHING IS FOILED 61

Chapter 16: MY CAREER BEGINS TO CHANGE.....................................63

Chapter 17: A BIG CHANGE...66

Chapter 18: STUNG BY A YELLOW JACKET 71

Chapter 19: SILLY ME 79

Chapter 20: DOCTOR OF RENAISSANCE MEDICINE 83

Chapter 21: UNDERCOVER 87

Chapter 22: A TASTE OF SUCCESS 90

Chapter 23: STUART SIDELINED 92

Chapter 24: I PINCH HIT FOR STUART 96

Chapter 25: THE WHISPER INN 98

Chapter 26: NECESSITY 101

Chapter 27: MY OWN HANDS 108

Chapter 28: TO THE RESCUE 110

Chapter 29: FRED THE PHILANDERER 122

Chapter 30: HETTA, HETTA MOON 125

Chapter 31: The Plot Thickens 128

Chapter 32: COMPLICATIONS 134

Chapter 33: HELP ARRIVES.. 136

Chapter 34: STUART CLEANS IT UP............................. 140

PROLOGUE

No one ever suspects me. I look like you'd remember your grandmother looking, but maybe with more modern clothes. And maybe not. I'm not a very fashionable dresser. Shopping is a chore, not a hobby, so I like clothes that last a long time and never look too dated. Of course, they never look very stylish, either. My hair is gradually fading from a plain medium brunette to the grayed brown of a field mouse. I'm at the age where mirrors startle me with their cruel reality – in my mind, my legs still stretch long and lean-muscled from a firm abdomen and a high, tight derriere. But I'm now the age that inspired manufacturers to add little strips of elastic, well-hidden but unmistakably there, to the waistbands of their conservatively-cut khaki slacks. Nevertheless, my skills are honed by life experience and, because I'm unexpected, I'm more dangerous than ever. When I want to be, anyway. Sometimes I bake cookies for a bunch of neighborhood kids. Then I'm grandmotherly, and only dangerous to their dental health and dinner appetites.

But sometimes I find out things that others want to keep secret.

My name is Hetta Moon. I think I'm still officially an administrative assistant.

Chapter 1

MY WORLD CHANGES

The doorbell rang. My husband Curly was working late and I was home by myself. So, although I am a little frightened of answering the door after dark, I set down my book and slid my feet back into the slippers I'd kicked off. I'm even more embarrassed to admit I'm frightened, so I always answer the door, even if I peek out the window or the peephole first.

Glancing at the clock, I noted it was pretty late for someone selling Girl Scout cookies or magazine subscriptions, and hoped it was just my neighbor, who'd locked himself out often enough that he'd given Curly and me keys to his house and to his car. I wish I could say I had a premonition, but instead of uneasiness, I was annoyed. The clock read twenty minutes past nine.

Where the hell was Curly, anyway?

The doorbell rang again, the brief press of a considerate friend instead of the longer buzz of a frustrated, locked-out neighbor.

I looked through the peephole in the door. Uniforms. Police uniforms. Two. That is never a good sign.

1

Smiling pleasantly, I opened the door.

"May I help you?" I asked.

One of the officers smiled slightly. I thought I recognized her. The other, the older man, looked solemn.

"May we come in?" the solemn officer said.

I knew that was definitely a bad sign.

And within ten minutes, I found out it was worse than I'd imagined. Much, much worse. I'd only imagined Curly dead.

Chapter 2

FOR THE WORSE

And that is how I found out my husband Curly had died. In circumstances that I couldn't have imagined. I knew Curly wasn't the perfect husband, but until his death I hadn't realized his imperfections went much beyond the old clichés of leaving the toilet seat up, abandoning dirty dishes throughout the house, and leaving bottle caps on the counter a mere two steps from the garbage can. I was stunned.

Curly worked for a giant insurance company as a bond investor. He decided where to put the money from premiums in order to make the most income before having to pay out claims. Curly was good at it, finding fairly high-yield yet low-risk investments with the uncanny talent of a truffle pig for finding rare fungus.

Since Curly's humiliating demise, I tend to think of him in terms of barnyard animals more often than I probably should. Maybe this is a sign of emotional distance, or stability, or something.

I think it's better than hiding and crying a lot, which I never did -- but sometimes I felt I should have.

Anyway, Curly managed our personal investments as carefully as the ones he handled professionally. I didn't mind picking up after him. I automatically checked every toilet seat I encountered without resentment or even resignation. After over two decades of marriage, I still liked Curly well enough and we had a comfortable life.

We worked at the same large company. I had taken an administrative position there shortly after our younger son entered his senior year of high school. Most of the time we commuted together.

At least, we had a comfortable life until Curly died and I found out the circumstances of his death from those two very embarrassed police officers. I should have suspected there was something fishy going on. But we'd been married twenty-six and a half years and had two grown children, so when Curly suggested we drive into work separately a couple of times a week so he could work late on a difficult project, I thought he was just being considerate. In the past, he'd told me to take a bus and then a cab from the bus stop when he occasionally stayed after normal working hours. I didn't appreciate it and wanted to rebel a little, but I didn't protest much and obediently took the bus and the cab. After raising our two sons through their teen years, I'd learned to pick my battles.

Driving myself twice a week was a treat. Not taking the bus and a cab saved me over an hour and I took that time to run errands or enjoy window-shopping at furniture or cooking stores, knowing Curly was busy.

Curly was a few years past fifty and we'd been driving on our new schedule for just a few weeks when he died of a heart attack. He died in a king-sized bed in a downtown hotel in the company of a pair of lithe blonde Slovakian contortionists -- identical twins -- from the "Circus of the Moon" traveling dance company. I just hadn't been expecting anything like that.

I told that to the very embarrassed police officers, that night in my living room, and they said they wouldn't have expected it, either. One of the officers, the younger one, had been in karate camp with our older son. She was obviously trying very hard to adopt a sympathetic manner. Her partner kept coughing into his hand. He was either coming down with something terrible or he hadn't done as well as his partner had in the Police Academy Sensitivity 101 class. I chose to believe he was getting a bad case of influenza. Later I wished that I had offered him an aspirin. But at the time I was too stunned to be bitchy.

Chapter 3

PIECES TO PICK UP

Our sons returned home for the funeral. Our older boy, Edward, is a fighter pilot with the Navy and we had to put off the service for a couple of days because he was out in the Pacific on an aircraft carrier. That was okay with me, because I'd had Curly's body cremated and ashes keep just fine. It gave me time to work out a suitable demeanor for myself (somewhere between outraged, deceived spouse and bereaved, loving wife) and a simple plan with the funeral home. I tried to get a cheap Slovakian-made casket to burn him in, but there weren't any. I settled for a plain pine casket and tucked a copy of a travel brochure featuring photos of Prague in with the body. The funeral director noticed, but managed to keep his face impassive. His son had played high school football with our younger son, so Curly and I knew him from games and sports banquets. I suppose he knew about the circumstances surrounding Curly's death. Everybody seemed to know.

By the time the boys arrived in town, I'd settled on smoldering, yet tightly controlled, anger laced with bitterness as my demeanor of choice. But I bought a hat with a dark veil anyway, so I could hide. I wasn't sure I could really keep my face under control. Jeff had always said he wanted to play poker with me, because my face read like a first-grade primer. Hence, the veil.

Our younger son Jeff was in a training camp for the Pittsburgh Steelers football team and working pretty hard, which was his excuse for arriving at the same time as Edward and not staying long after the funeral. I, of course, assured both of them that I'd be fine and had a strong support group of friends and neighbors.

I think they were really just pretty uncomfortable with the circumstances of their father's death, which I had not discussed with them. I really didn't know how to tell them without humiliating myself beyond what I felt I could bear. But I'm sure they found out quickly, probably before they'd set foot in the house. We live in one of those small bedroom communities outside of Hartford, Connecticut, and news this juicy is hard to keep quiet. Especially when everyone pretends, really hard, that it shouldn't be discussed.

After the funeral, which was quite short as no one wanted to speak very long about what a fine family man Curly had been, we stowed Curly's ashes in a marble cupboard in a cemetery. I had thought about renting a locker in a big city bus terminal, knowing that I wouldn't really do that. But I certainly enjoyed thinking about it. With all the concerns about terrorism, these lockers aren't that common anymore. And, when you can find them, they don't have long-term rental arrangements. Even if I could have found a locker, I wasn't ready to commit to frequent mandatory visits to insert more coins, so I gave up that idea with a mixture of relief and disappointment. I wasn't interested in a double plot in the Garden of Grief, either, and decided if I changed my mind and wanted to keep my earthly remains next to that cheating bastard's for all eternity, two boxes of ashes could be stacked and fit just fine in the little cubby. I didn't discuss any of this with the boys.

I also did not discuss the circumstances surrounding their father's death beyond telling them flatly that he had succumbed to a heart attack and I hadn't been with him. They did not press me for details, which proved to me that they had heard the lurid details from another source. After all, they grew up in the town and knew plenty of people.

I had tried to invite the Slovakian contortionists to the funeral, but the Circus of the Moon had left town and I didn't try all that hard, which was probably a good thing. I would have had to explain their presence to Edward and Jeff. I wore sunglasses around town, and my new hat with the veil to the funeral, so that people would think I was crying even though I usually wasn't.

The day after the service, Jeff kissed me awkwardly and hugged me tightly before he left. He's a wide receiver, or was for four years at the University of Connecticut, and his tight hugs are like a barrier against all bad things, and more effective than mocha chip ice cream, my usual cure for a bad day.

As I was remaining in the house, there was no need for a lot of clean-up, so I waved good-bye to Edward two days later. I spent the next week bagging Curly's clothes into big black plastic garbage bags and hauling them to the closest charity to fill in the hours between meetings with the attorney and insurance professionals to address the endless paperwork. One time, I collected three large bags of Curly's clothes, two bags of his favorite snack foods, a bag of the paperback books that he liked, and another bag full of his toiletries and other possibly useful personal items. I tucked in various bits of jewelry that Curly had given me – or not given me - including two identical gold bangle bracelets that I found, wrapped separately, in the bottom of his sock drawer and which I somehow did NOT think were meant for me. I tied up the bags, loaded them in my plain sedan, and drove to the old railroad overpass on the north side of

8

Hartford. There, I unloaded the offerings in the middle of a homeless community which had recently been featured in the Sunday paper. The people there watched me, both cautious and curious. One man, bolder than the others, began opening the bags before I'd pulled my car back onto the road.

Curly's estate was simple, with almost everything in both our names, but even the relative simplicity of transferring Curly's possessions consumed a whole grove of trees. Throughout, I wondered why he'd cheated on me, and tried to think of plausible reasons for his death scenario. My imagination, though usually quite lively, had withered and offered me no explanations, at any level of plausibility, other than the obvious. I wanted to miss my husband, but I was too hurt, and mostly in whatever anatomical area houses pride.

Luckily, between insurance and investments Curly had left me financially very well off. Our house, a rambling ranch with rooms and hallways leading to more rooms sticking out in all directions, boasted a front porch, a stone patio, an enviable location and an even more enviable zero balance on the mortgage. I held title to Curly's tan Mercedes, which looked to me like an expensive cigar box with wheels and a shiny finish. I also had my little four-door sedan, which I found much more comfortable to drive. I hate worrying about parking lot scratches and coffee drips, so I always insisted on a modest car with a reputation for reliability. During the third week after Curly's death, I sold the Mercedes and bought a new, bright red Mustang convertible with a leather interior and a manual transmission. If I was going to worry about parking lot scratches and coffee drips in a car, it was going to be worth the worry. A tan Mercedes wasn't. A red Mustang most certainly was.

Chapter 4

DROPPING SOME PIECES

After three weeks, I went back to work at the insurance company. This was not my wisest decision, ranking even below trying to invite the Slovakian contortionists to Curly's funeral. In a big corporation, rumors run rampant between departments and exotic contortionist twins are hard to squelch. When I heard whispers that I had been involved along with a spider monkey and a French horn, I stayed late one night, typed up a resignation letter giving two weeks' notice and left it on my boss's desk, centered on the blotter and held in place with a letter opener shaped like a small sword. I resisted the impulse to use the letter opener like a dagger and impale my letter on the blotter. Then I made four dozen photocopies of the police report – with NO mention of me and absolutely NO mention of a French horn OR a spider monkey. The report did, however, contain the added and to me totally unnecessary information that the contortionists were blonde identical twins aged 31 years old. I grabbed a staple gun I'd brought from home and posted these copies on every bulletin board I could find, plus directly on some walls when the bulletin boards seemed too far apart. Then I went back to my boss's desk and stuck the letter opener through my resignation letter and into the blotter. The blotter was too thin to hold the letter opener vertical, so the dramatic effect was lost. I burst into tears and left.

I called in sick the next morning and my boss assured me that I did not need to give further notice. He sounded more horrified than sympathetic, and I wondered idly if he and the snickering policeman who'd notified me of Curly's passing were somehow related. Maybe they'd both just failed the same Sympathy 101 class.

After a month at home I decided I needed a job. I'd repainted every room in the house with a different lively color and experimented with "accent walls" in two rooms (Curly had insisted on white walls everywhere, as they were easier to maintain). Most of the furniture had been newly reupholstered in bright chintz or canvas fabrics, because I like bright colors and Curly had always insisted on neutrals. I'd also baked and mailed three batches of cookies to both Edward and Jeff, triggering a phone call from Jeff asking me not to get too enthusiastic on the pastries and reminding me that he was in training, and so was the rest of his team, so he couldn't even just share the excess goodies. I'd taken to standing sentry in the garden, hoe in hand, waiting for a weed to pop up. That's when it hit me: I needed something to do. Fast.

I made a cup of tea, grabbed a pen and pad and opened the paper to the classified ads. A week later, I'd graduated to a pot of tea and the internet and still hadn't found a job. Even volunteer jobs for someone with my skills involved way too much social interaction. It would be like working at the insurance company, with whispers and averted eyes. I'd work for real and donate my wages: volunteerism without the human interaction.

After two weeks of searching, I was beginning to give up hope. I just couldn't face working as a receptionist in a real estate office where everyone would chat and new residents were bursting with curiosity about their town. Retail, same problem. I was considering working as a home care companion, but didn't feel I could remain kind and patient for more than fifteen minutes or so at a time. I paced around the house and yard, reluctant to even go around the block unless I was inside a car and somewhat barricaded from my neighbors. There were no weeds in the garden and the entire house gleamed, even the windows. I'd shampooed the cat, who now glared at me suspiciously and refused my conciliatory offers of head pats. And I was having no luck with the job hunt. It was a bad day, a very, very bad day.

Chapter 5

ICE CREAM THERAPY WORKS

An extremely bad day calls for mocha chip ice cream from Sweet Melissa's. Of course, extremely good days call for mocha chip ice cream from Sweet Melissa's, too, which is probably why I go there. Maybe subconsciously I think I can trick myself into believing the extremely bad days are really extremely good days if I go deeply enough into frozen-sugar-and-cream heaven. Sweet Melissa's makes all the ice cream on the premises, and until recently even featured two flavors made with real alcohol (their rum raisin had a genuine kick). Sweet Melissa is really a sixty-year-old half-Mexican and half-Cajun man named Jorge Carl DuBois with five grandchildren and a wife, Murriel, who works as the town clerk. Jorge decided it wasn't worth having to card every teen-ager who came in after a baseball game and discontinued the adult flavors. Now Jorge experiments with candy and fruit and nuts instead of the contents of his liquor cabinet.

Today, Sweet Melissa was out of mocha chip ice cream. I paced in front of the case, adjusting my sunglasses and searching vainly. It's a short case. Sweet Melissa's stocks a dozen or so flavors at any time. Usually mocha chip is available because it's Murriel's favorite, and Jorge is still, after forty years of marriage, dotty about Murriel.

Sweet Melissa's was crowded. A line twisted around the tables inside and stretched out the door. A lot of parents with children in rumpled and dirty Little League uniforms milled around the counter. I'd picked a bad time to apply the Sweet Melissa's treatment to my extremely bad day.

"Sweet Melissa," I addressed Jorge, when it was finally my turn at the counter. He laughs, usually, when I call him that, but I think it really busts his balls. Which is my intention today. He's out of mocha chip, so he deserves that and more. "Where is the mocha chip ice cream? Did Murriel eat her way through the entire batch without my help?"

"Murriel is visiting her sister in Louisiana for two weeks," smiles Jorge. Really, he's giving me more of a grimace. He's actually just baring his teeth. I'll bet I'm not the first person who called him "Sweet Melissa" today. "I took a break from making it and invented 'Starry Night' instead."

"I'm Melissa," chimed in one of the two perky teen-agers working behind the counter with him. She was scooping "Polka Dot" ice cream into a stubby waffle cone shaped like a dish. Sweet Melissa's doesn't use plastic containers except for take-out, substituting substantial waffle cones of various shapes, with a napkin surrounding the outside (in a nod to hygiene), for dishes. I think Melissa is trying to distract Jorge, who is probably tired of the "Sweet Melissa" joke and frazzled from the long line at the counter and, probably most of all, from Murriel's absence.

"I'm Hetta," I chirped back at Melissa, trying to imitate her perkiness, only with an added dash of bitchiness. I glanced at the description of the new flavor on the label card. It was a dark chocolate base with a lot of light-colored stuff in it, like

14

marshmallows and white chocolate chips and macadamia nuts and dried pineapple bits. "I'll take a small cone of 'Starry Night' with a cherry on top," I say to Jorge. But I scowl to show my protest over the lack of mocha chip.

I like a cherry on top because it sounds happy. I don't particularly like maraschino cherries, but it's all part of fooling myself into believing that it's an extremely good day.

Cherries are not meant to balance on top of rounded scoops of ice cream, but to nestle in beds of whipped cream and marshmallow fluff, or perhaps cling to sticky hot fudge or caramel. I should have been better prepared. But I wasn't, and I'm glad now. When I turned to leave, I bumped into a young man in the crowd. My cherry wobbled and started to fall. A strong, young and very male hand darted out and snatched the fruit as it began to tumble to the floor.

"Oops," I said.

"Gotcha!" said the owner of the successful hand. The hand opened. My maraschino cherry nestled securely, if stickily, in a palm that was as well-muscled as any I'd ever seen. Although I hadn't before inspected palms for muscularity, this one made me seriously consider what I've been missing.

I followed the brawny arm attached to the hand with my eyes, past a well-formed shoulder and up to a chiseled jaw. I looked past a cheeky grin and into a pair of dark blue eyes fringed with improbably thick lashes.

"Your cherry?" he inquired, and then his grin disappeared and his pale face flushed a brick red. "Very young," I thought. "And right now probably very horrified."

"Thank you," I said, and plucked it from his palm. I raised an eyebrow at his blush and grinned in a manner I hoped could be described as "saucy" and not "maniacal." Without further ado, I turned and made my way through the crowd. Tormenting young men with awkward and insincere and improbable flirtations was beneath me. But I mentally catalogued a list of clever responses that, if I had less dignity, I'd have enjoyed out loud. I absent-mindedly popped the cherry in my mouth. I said I don't particularly like maraschino cherries, but I don't particularly dislike them, either. And I was too bemused with embarrassing a handsome young man, even without intending to, to be paying attention to the hygienic issue of eating a maraschino cherry manhandled by the aforementioned handsome young man.

I found a lawn chair among the mismatched collection outside. Jorge kept chairs and tables scattered across two patios and a lawn sporting at least two dozen rhododendron bushes and a couple of shade trees. Jorge and Murriel lived above Sweet Melissa's in an apartment that I hoped smelled constantly of vanilla and custard and was decorated in a lively mix of Mexican and Cajun styles. I'd never seen it, but I liked to imagine it while I took the cure for a very bad day. The evening was coming to a close and dusk settled over the bushes with little samples of the coming night tucked beneath each bush. A couple of fireflies signaled to potential mates.

A strong, young, male hand pulled a chair next to mine. It was a familiar strong, young, male hand.

"Want an unblemished cherry?" asked a strong, young, male voice. I followed a familiar arm past a familiar well-formed shoulder and jaw and ended at a set of smiling eyes. Not a young man to remain embarrassed for long, I noted.

"Thank you," I said, nodding my head slightly, and plucked the fruit from the top of what appeared to be a peach-with-raspberry-swirl cone, held toward me in invitation. I was not one to be shy any longer about well-formed jaws and deep blue eyes, especially ones that were young enough to belong to my children's classmates. But I could enjoy them, and I did, while projecting nonchalance.

"Sorry to run into you earlier," said Strong Jaw And Deep Blue Eyes as he folded himself into the slightly-too-small lawn chair. He appeared to have recovered admirably from his earlier embarrassment.

"I thought I jostled you," I said. He smiled.

"My name's Mitch." He held out that strong, young male hand, and I shook it.

"Hetta. Hetta Moon," I said.

"Nice evening," said Mitch, staring across the lawn and licking his cone.

"Much improved by ice cream."

"One of those days, huh?"

"Sweet Melissa's is either a cure or a celebration, and today it's a cure," I explained, licking my cone and looking into the darkening distance. After all, I was never going to see this stranger again, so I could speak freely. And it was getting dark, which always seems to encourage an easy exchange of confidences.

"Same here," said Mitch. "I got another letter from my mother indicating that either I should be disemboweled or disinherited or both, or else she's going off the deep end again."

"How unfortunate." Ah, I was to determine his guilt or innocence regarding his mother's accusations. Being roughly her age, I probably struck Mitch as a suitable judge and jury. I decided to offer any absolution Mitch required. After all, he gave me his cherry after saving mine. I grinned inwardly, keeping my face impassive. Or at least expressionless enough to pass in the gathering twilight. Someday I might drift into some vague mental state related to age, or pretend to drift into it, and enjoy shocking others with every thought that passed through my mind. But I wasn't starting today. I'd keep my racy thoughts to myself.

"That's why I live here while my mother lives, well, far away."

"Wise," I approved, bringing my attention back to the conversation. "Could be hormones," I added.

"Could be," Mitch agreed, and stroked his ice cream with a tongue that, by golly, looked muscular.

17

"Worth a check," I said.

"Oh, yes." Mitch licked contemplatively for a moment. "Have you ever wondered what their apartment is like? Jorge and Murriel's?"

"I hope colorful and with a lovely aroma." My brief comment seemed to satisfy Mitch's need for understanding, and he was ready to move on.

"I always think it must be like a fantasy. Like a Maxfield Parrish painting."

"Ah," I murmured. Mitch knows who Maxfield Parrish is. How unusual for a young man. I try not to underestimate handsome young men, but sometimes I do.

"What do you think?"

"I always fancied a lot of red and yellow and blue, with a stuffed alligator someplace. Sort of show her Cajun roots and his Mexican and Cajun roots. And smelling like vanilla."

"That would be like a fantasy."

"Yes."

"Probably all beige and brown plaid."

"Probably. But that would be disappointing."

"So we keep our fantasies."

"Absolutely," I agreed.

We licked at our cones in a companionable silence for a few minutes. I was pondering whether Mitch thought this was a deep conversation.

"What is a good day like for you?" asked Mitch.

"Justice prevails," I said, without thinking.

"You a cop?"

"Nope. I'd just like some justice." Suddenly I felt dangerously close to the tears that I'd yet to shed for Curly. Only these weren't for Curly, either. These were for me, and my futile job search and my imagined future highlighted by putting together scrap books of Jeff's football career and putting pins on maps where I thought

18

Edward might be flying. Maybe I'd start hoarding newspapers and collecting cats.

Mitch looked at me, and I hoped my threatening tears stayed hidden.

"I bake cookies," I offered rather lamely.

"That's a handy skill. Professionally?"

"No, recreationally. I'm only really good at three kinds. What makes a good day for you?" I took a deep breath to control the tears and wished I'd kept my sunglasses on. But I'd put them in my purse when I was paying for my ice cream. I hadn't expected to run into anyone who would be expecting me to cry. Or anyone who would be expecting me not to cry. Or anyone at all.

"A good day for me involves eating cookies," Mitch smiled, and then shrugged. "A good day is when everything works."

"Oh," I said, trying to sound inquisitive.

"I restore cars and work on equipment. And sometimes motorcycles. And other stuff."

"So a bad day means…"

"Things stay broken."

"Oh."

"I can usually fix things. But sometimes it takes a while to find out what needs fixing."

"I see." We both crunched into our cones.

"What you do is detective work, then – of a sort."

"That makes it sound more exciting. But it's more like just a logic puzzle, you know?" Mitch seemed to forget his ice cream. "So many people just keep battering at the same thing if there's a problem, thinking that if an action seems like it should solve the problem, they just have to keep doing the same thing. That's not how mechanical things work. Cars, computers, motorcycles, locks - they don't change their minds and suddenly work. You have to try something new, look in a new place, check it out from a new angle. Sometimes you need a fresh perspective. It's a logic puzzle." Mitch put his attention back onto his ice cream cone, which had begun to drip down his hand. I casually watched him lick his hand. A hand with lots of muscles. Just like his other hand.

I looked at Mitch's face. "Interesting."

"I think so," agreed Mitch.

"I'm looking for clerical work at a small place," I ventured. Maybe I needed to try something other than classified advertisements; maybe I needed a new angle. Maybe Mitch was one of those angels who are always being written up in supermarket tabloids. Maybe I was on a sugar high from the ice cream.

"You're a new widow, right?"

"Why?" Instantly suspicious, probably from the sugar high, I wanted to say "What's it to you?" but that sounded overly hostile.

"You have a ring indentation on your left ring finger." I examined my left hand. Not only did I have a deep, pale indentation on my ring finger, but I had a callous on the palm side of my finger, on each side of where a long-worn wedding ring would sit.

"Well done, Sherlock." I was impressed. I was also impressed by the size of my ring calluses, which I hadn't really noticed before this.

"And I recognized your name." Mitch looked sheepish.

"Oh." I was much less impressed. And much more embarrassed. He probably knew about the Slovakian contortionists. After all, pretty much everybody did. Maybe there were some preschoolers or dementia patients tucked into corners of Hartford County who hadn't heard about Curly and the twins. Maybe.

"May I speak freely?"

"I can always leave," I assured him, and finished off my cone. I was ready to dash off if Slovakia or twins or especially contortionists came up as topics.

"If you want justice to prevail, my neighbor runs a private investigator firm and he needs a part-time receptionist. He doesn't know he does yet, but he does. Can you type?"

"I'm a woman of mature years. Of course I can type. And file, and spell, and I know phone etiquette." I sniffed slightly. It wasn't because I was offended, but because I was fighting back those tears again. Mitch was looking more and more like a tabloid angel. "I even know how to use a dictionary, and my grammar is quite passable."

"Go see him. Derek Irons Agency. You'll want to see Stuart Wilkins. Just stop by. Mention my name."

"Mitch -?"

"Gallifianakis. But just Mitch will do," he grinned. Mitch finished his cone. "Stuart is not very well organized. Good luck. This could be a real good match."

I didn't understand his last comment until I looked down at my lap. I'd automatically folded and stacked my three used paper napkins. Mitch saw me grab the napkins and crumple them. He rose, smiled at me and held out his hand.

"Best of luck to you," he said as we shook hands, slightly stickily. "And thanks for reassuring me that not every 'woman of mature years,' as you put it, wants to classify me as the crowning exhibit in the Museum of Bad Young Men."

"My pleasure," I assured him, although I didn't understand, at the time, why he should consider himself even eligible for exhibition in the Museum of Bad Young Men. And, with a promising job lead handed to me, I wasn't paying enough attention to be curious.

Chapter 6

DEREK IRONS

The next day, a Friday, I went to the Derek Irons Agency. I'd found the address on the internet, and checked what information I could find. It wasn't much, and I know very little about private investigators, but I felt ready to go to the office and meet Mr. Irons.

I arrived at 10 AM. I thought nine o'clock looked too eager, maybe even to the point of needy. Later in the day and I risked an empty office on a Friday with nice weather. Or a Friday night of tracking criminals who were "working late" and meeting paramours and drug lords, I thought, adjusting my thinking to accommodate the vague ideas of private investigators I'd gleaned from television and Curly's favorite paperback thrillers. The thrillers that were now entertaining the homeless under the railroad overpass.

The office address was for an old department store that had been turned into a little strip mall with offices on the second floor. The building tried to be trendy but verged on shabby in spite of the art deco architecture. The sign listing the businesses looked dated. The building sat between a gas station and a dry cleaner/tailor shop.

I stepped through spacious doors into a deep and narrow marble-floored entrance hall that had obviously been walled in from much more spacious dimensions. Various signs carelessly dotted the sand-colored walls. I read that I was not allowed to smoke, litter, post bills or solicit. A grooved black board with little white plastic letters that could be rearranged as tenants changed announced that "Derek Irons Ag ncy" was on the "2 d flo r" in room 204. I climbed a set of elegantly curved stairs, also marble, that incongruously originated next to a row of flimsy-looking locked mailboxes. The second floor was obviously adapted from a partial mezzanine, with thin walls partitioning off various small offices for bookkeepers and temporary worker agencies. I found the door for Derek Irons, PI, and knocked. The translucent glass door panel showed me a light was on inside, and I opened the door without waiting for an answer. I was eager to face what Mitch seemed to consider my destiny. Actually, I was eager to face any sort of excitement that didn't involve Curly and Slovakians.

At first I thought opening the door must have triggered a silent explosion. There were papers and books and folders and files everywhere. Three filing cabinets lined one wall, and four of the 15 drawers were open. Papers stuck out of the others. Stacks of papers were arranged on the floor. I amended my first impression. It would have had to have been a very organized explosion to leave so many of the papers in even such rough stacks.

Another door burst open, and a small, sandy-haired, balding man charged into the room. He couldn't be much over thirty years old. I thought maybe Derek Irons had already hired an office assistant.

"MayIhelpyou?" the man asked, breathlessly.

"Mitch sent me." I extended a hand.

He adjusted his polo shirt with the palms of his hands, which made me think he was really wiping sweat off his palms, adjusted his glasses and took my hand in a surprisingly hearty and surprisingly dry handshake.

"Stuart Wilkins, Senior Investigator of the Derek Irons PI Agency at your service," he said.

"Hetta Moon, hopefully at your service," I responded, and looked around. "Did Mitch mention me?"

"Are you here for investigative services?" Stuart asked.

"No. Did Mitch mention me?" I repeated. Stuart seemed a bit scattered, so I wanted to focus his attention. I stared at him really hard, but stopped short of cupping his face between my hands and asking him to focus on me. I used to do that with a neighbor's golden retriever when they were on vacation and left him with me. It had worked pretty well with the dog, so I thought I'd hold it in reserve as an option for Stuart.

"He called me this morning and said I needed an angel and he may have found one. Is that you?"

"I hope so." I looked around. Or maybe I didn't hope so. "Do you have a job opening?"

"Not really," Stuart hesitated. "Maybe. What do you do?"

"I type, file, answer phones and bill clients. Do you need these services?"

"Yes."

"Do you want these services?" Stuart glanced wildly around the room. Maybe he was trying to escape. "Focus!" I commanded, without thinking. I very nearly grabbed his head, but stopped myself.

"Yes!" he barked.

"Shall we have an interview?"

"Mitch sent you, so no."

"When do I start?"

"What are your terms?"

"Let's have a look at the books and we'll see what you can afford, OK?" I was starting to feel like this was a crusade. "Do you turn in philandering husbands so that betrayed wives can get well-deserved divorces and decent settlements?"

"Yes…" Stuart hesitated again.

"Then I'll start now, and today will be a test to see if we work out well. No pay, no promises. Then we can talk about details." I waved away insignificant details like hourly wage, overtime, and benefits like so many mosquitoes. After all, I was well set financially. I needed… something else. A purpose. Justice. Something.

"OK," said Stuart, and I grabbed a pile of documents off the floor before what sounded like hesitation on his part developed into something that sounded like refusal.

Chapter 7

A POSSIBILITY

By 1:30 pm I had two file drawers organized and a list of office supplies that we'd need. Mostly folders and labels, with some fasteners and a big calendar. And I needed lunch, or I'd start getting crabby.

"Stuart?"

"Yes?" Stuart stumbled from the back room, where I had seen him hunched over a computer. He'd been alternately typing madly and leaning back, stretching, mumbling and messing up his hair for about three hours. I had no idea what he was doing.

"As a Gal Friday, where do I get sandwiches?"

Stuart blinked.

The phone rang, for the first time since I arrived. I answered, as I was closer to the front room extension than he was to either phone. And I wanted to show off my receptionist skills.

"Derek Irons, Private Investigations. May I help you?" I enunciated clearly, glancing at Stuart.

A female voice growled a request for Mr. Irons himself. Since I hadn't seen him yet, I envisioned him out in a scuba suit sneaking onto a yacht full of diamond smugglers, maybe even in Candlewood Lake. But that was an unlikely place for diamond smugglers, so I amended my vision to relocate the adventurous Mr. Irons to Long Island Sound.

"I'm sorry, Mr. Irons is not available. May I take a message or may someone else help you?"

The voice asked for someone, anyone, who could catch her philandering, cheating, BASTARD of a stupid husband with his cheap whore so she could divorce his sorry ass without losing control of the business that SHE really runs and he'd just destroy if it wasn't for her tireless efforts. Then the voice paused to take a breath.

I thought she deserved help, based on that synopsis of the situation.

"May I have your name, please?" I tried to sound both sympathetic and professional. I was a little tempted to compare notes with her. I thought my philandering, cheating bastard of a stupid husband would trump hers, and maybe she'd feel better. But I knew that gossiping at the reception desk with prospective clients wasn't professional behavior, so I choked back my commiseration.

"Oh." The voice on the phone quieted immediately. "I'm sorry. I'm Millie Robertson."

"Let me see if Mr. Wilkins is available," I responded, all efficiency. I pressed "hold" and covered the phone, too, because I'm very careful.

"Pissed off wife," I explained. "Philandering husband, and she wants his balls on a plate."

I thought I sounded hard-boiled and tough, like I belonged on this team.

Stuart raised a beige eyebrow and handed me the bill he had just fished out of his wallet. "Monterey Jack-style soy cheese with sprouts and mustard on a whole-wheat pita, and carrot juice. Get whatever you want, too. There's a health food store with a deli three doors past the dry cleaner. It's called 'The Healthy Belly Deli.'" Stuart winced slightly as he said the name.

I traded him the phone for the money, grabbed my purse and waved as I ducked out of the office. As I closed the door, I heard him answer the phone.

"This is Stu Wilkins. How may I help you?" His voice, disconnected from his physical appearance, was deep and resonant. Stuart Wilkins sounded like he could wrestle alligators and come out with a set of luggage and a pair of shoes. Stuart Wilkins *looked* like he could disappear in a crowd of two. I pondered the dichotomy of Stuart Wilkins as I counted the doors past the dry cleaner's.

The deli catered to young, health-conscious professionals and advertised that by being totally made of pale knotty pine. There was no salami and no diet soda, but "organic" was shouted from almost every sign. I settled for a roast veggie wrap and a bottle of water. I let Stuart treat me. Although I'd started feeling maternal, sorting his papers and watching him ruffle his wispy pale hair as he hunched over a computer screen, his voice as I left made me think that my instincts may have been misplaced.

When I returned, bearing sandwiches, Stuart grinned broadly.

"I was afraid you wouldn't come back," he told me.

It was my turn to raise an eyebrow as I handed him the deli bag, after removing my wrap and bottle of water.

"You think I'd bail for the price of two lunches?" I asked.

"No. I thought maybe you were a vision and would disappear. Look at this office!" he crowed.

I looked at the office. It looked like a really, really messy office that someone had tried valiantly — and almost, but not quite, fruitlessly - to organize for about three hours.

"Yeah?" I said.

"This is the BEST it's looked in a while," Stuart said, and sank to the floor clutching the deli bag. He crossed his legs in a yoga position, closed his eyes and took a deep breath, letting it out slowly.

"Is there a place I can wash my hands?" I asked, eyeing a suspiciously solid and unopened door.

"Bathroom's down the hall. The key's on the hook below the light switch. That's the storage closet for old files."

I wondered how he knew what I was thinking. Stuart's eyes were still closed; he couldn't have seen my glance.

"And the storage closet is empty," Stuart continued.

"Good," I said, and left for the washroom.

It was clean, but ugly with worn porcelain fixtures in a shade of pink that hadn't been fashionable for over a generation and well-aged linoleum flooring in beige, pink and gold. I didn't care. It didn't have papers stacked all over it, like the office, so it was a welcome relief, aesthetically speaking, and it had running water and soap.

When I returned, Stuart was in an awkward pose that had probably started with him lying on his back. His feet touched the floor above his head, and a knee rested near each ear. He was humming "Happy Birthday."

I sat at the desk, which would serve as a receptionist's desk, should Stuart not frighten off any potential receptionists and any potential clients, and cleared off an area to serve as a lunch space. Just for me. Stuart was on his own.

I unwrapped my lunch as Stuart unfolded on the floor.

"Ah," sighed Stuart, and went out the door. He left the deli bag in the middle of the floor. I started to feel maternal again, but not in a good way.

Stuart returned as I was beginning to crave a good cup of tea. Or a cup of strong, black, private-eye-style coffee.

"This is wonderful," he said, gesturing around the room.

"Here's your change," I said, instantly amending my attitude and beaming, and handed him the coins returned from lunch.

"Put it in the coffee fund," Stuart said.

"Coffee fund?" I asked, hopefully. Maybe there was coffee someplace around here?

"We need one, don't we? There's a coffee machine around here someplace. I just never bother for just me."

Silly me, when Stuart said that I just assumed that Derek Irons, mysterious private eye, was out a lot. Or didn't drink coffee.

"How are you with bookkeeping?" said Stuart, as he sank to the floor by the deli bag.

"OK. Actually, better than that. I'm pretty good," I admitted. I'd organized financial records for the department I'd covered in the big insurance company.

"After lunch, we open the books," promised Stuart, rooting for his sandwich among the brown paper napkins.

And so we did. And we discovered, to my surprise but not to Stuart's, that the Derek Irons PI Agency could definitely afford a Gal Friday – or even two, but I figured one would suffice if that one was me. When I asked Stuart if Derek needed to be consulted, he looked at me like I'd swallowed a goldfish without being dared. He assured me that wouldn't be necessary and that anything he pushed for would be approved. He pulled out a couple of forms and asked me to complete them for his records. I knew enough already to consider that optimistic of him, since without me I wasn't sure he'd ever find any of his papers again. I was a bit nonplussed when he confidently moved to a tall stack on top of a bookshelf and pulled another file from it, about three inches from the top, with barely a pause.

"Here are the government forms I'll need you to fill out for tax purposes. You handle them. Part of your duties."

I accepted the file. We completed our negotiations for salary and hours in just a few minutes because I didn't negotiate at all. I just took what he offered. Stuart asked me to return on Tuesday morning to begin my real employment. He added that, if there was a problem, he'd call me.

Chapter 8

I WAIT AND SHOP FOR BLACK LEATHER PANTS

I spent Saturday washing windows. I scrubbed and polished them inside and out, including the screens. I laundered and ironed all the curtains, which I re-hung on newly polished curtain rods. I called Becky. I'd known her since we were both newlyweds in the same neighborhood. A Southern girl with natural charm and raised to be a lady, she had been desperately trying to adjust to New England weather, a new marriage, and Yankee ways. Our children grew up together, and my Edward briefly dated her Carmen until they both decided it was too much like incest and amicably dissolved the lackluster, but comfortable, almost-romance.

"Busy this evening? I've got a bottle of Vino Verde, some lovely brie, and news," I opened the conversation.

Ah'd love to," answered Becky eagerly. "Howie has his bowling league tonight and they are getting ready for a tournament next weekend, so he'll be busy for hours. Can Ah have a sneak preview of this news?"

"I may have a job. With a private investigation agency. I'll find out Monday and I'm a little nervous…"

"Why, you certainly need company tonight in your hour of need. Howie will just have to go bowling without me in the cheering section. A PI office, huh? Sounds quite exciting. Is this from that nice and handsome young man at Sweet Melissa's?" I had told Becky everything.

"Yeah, this was his lead. It's a strange place, but I think I can be useful and it will get me out of the house."

"This sounds lovely. Ah have been just a bit concerned that you will paint your bathroom red and put in disco lights if you fail to get a better hobby right quick. Listen, Sugah, I need to check on the meatloaf in the oven and prepare Howie for this evening's athletic endeavahs. He has to be at the bowling alley by six. I'll be over as soon as I send him off." Becky kissed into the phone and hung up.

Over a bottle of Portuguese Vino Verde and a plate of sesame crackers, creamy brie, and grapes, we discussed our children for a few minutes. After exchanging updates, I told her about my new job -- or, rather, my potential new job.

"Honey," drawled Becky (she'd never completely lost her Alabama roots, and when she was excited, or drinking wine, Becky slipped deeper into her accent), "this is so exciting! Chasing down jewel thieves! Maybe even involved in intahnational intrigue!"

"I think I'll be filing papers," I said dryly, and re-filled her wine glass.

"We need ta buy yew a paih of black boots with heels. And a paih of leathah pants," Becky continued. "Black leathah pants."

I've known Becky a long time. I knew she was having fun with this by the way she liberally sugared her vowels and dropped her "r"s, and I decided to enjoy the fantasy, too. We finished the bottle of wine while searching for "black leather pants" on the desktop computer in Curly's study. We found a lot of websites that weren't selling clothing, and sent us into fits of screaming laughter until one site's advertisement featured two matching blond women in nothing but tiny leather shorts and I turned off the computer. Becky fumbled around in her enormous handbag and fished out a glossy catalogue and a bottle of California pinot noir she'd tucked in for our evening's entertainment. Another glass of wine each and we ended up on the phone, trying to order black leather jeans in my size. Luckily, the most likely fit was on backorder and I sobered up enough to cancel the order, claiming I couldn't wait the extra six weeks. The pants probably wouldn't fit right anyway; they didn't have an elastic inset waistband.

"Boots?" Becky suggested.

"Movie," I countered.

"James Bond." Becky was adamant. That was fine with me. Curly had a collection of every James Bond movie ever made, and I never remembered any one of them. Between Curly and our two boys, these movies had been the backbone of our home video collection. I hadn't gotten rid of them yet. I thought maybe one of the boys would take them.

"An early one, with Sean Connery," I insisted. I could be adamant, too.

We ended up watching the one with a group of women pilots, led by Pussy Galore. I'd read an interview with Sean Connery in some magazine in a doctor's or dentist's office somewhere. He'd said that all the actors had to practice saying "Pussy Galore" without giggling, and it wasn't easy. I liked the movie because of that, and I always checked to see if any of the actors was caught smirking uncontrollably on camera. Becky, fueled by the Vino Verde, helped me look. We giggled, probably because of the wine, every time anyone said "Pussy Galore" in the movie. When there were spells where no one referred to the intrepid woman pilot, we said it ourselves and burst into giggles. When the wine wore off, we still giggled.

Becky thought I needed breeches and a white men's-style shirt after watching the movie, but I pointed out I wasn't a pilot and I wasn't a spy and I wasn't a private investigator. I was a receptionist. The plain skirts, slacks, sweaters and simple blouses I'd worn in my job at the insurance company would be more than adequate for my new duties.

We talked some more about my new job. Becky suggested it was good that I'd have an outside interest in a place where I could start the rumors, instead of in a big company where I had little or no control over them. I told her she was very insightful. Around 10:30 she left, explaining Howard was coming home soon and she'd have to console him if he hadn't won a bowling trophy, and admire him if he did. I wondered how much admiration a bowling trophy warranted, but I didn't say anything. Sometimes I'm smart like that.

On Sunday, I rattled around for a couple of hours, unable to settle with a book or television or another movie. I took a long walk, and decided I needed to start an exercise program to make sure I was strong enough for any grueling adventures I'd encounter in my new job. Like having two calls come in at once.

Twenty minutes later, I'd run through all the calisthenics I remembered from high school gym classes. I couldn't do more than one push-up, even with my knees on the floor. There was something I'd read, maybe in line at a supermarket check-out, about deep knee bends being bad for aging joints, so I skipped those. I felt silly. I decided I didn't need an exercise program to be a receptionist, no matter what kind of office I was serving. I told myself I was sadly confusing private investigators -- and their receptionists -- with secret agents. And not even real secret agents, who nobody really knows about anyway because they are secret, but Hollywood-style secret agents.

I spent the rest of the day on the internet looking into information about private investigators in Connecticut and what they did. I wasn't sure what to believe. Even seemingly official websites could be suspect, as I'd found. I'd been fooled in the past into collecting a couple of nasty computer viruses when I followed links from sites that looked legitimate. Every once in a while I make macaroni and cheese and cookies for one of Edward's friends who still lives in the area and can do magical things with personal computers. He cleans up my computer systems and gives me a little tutorial. I'm never allowed to pay him for his wizardry. He accepts nothing but my undying gratitude, dinner, and little plastic containers of leftovers to take home. He'd taught me what "cookies" are in the world of computers, so we always make bad jokes about him removing cookies from my house, and only some of them being chocolate chip. So, mindful of my brief lessons on avoiding computer troubles, I didn't follow up on the websites with flashing lights or lots of exclamation points. The others didn't promise much enlightenment on the life of a private investigator, so I learned very little.

Chapter 9

SELECTED AS A GAL FRIDAY

On Monday, I completed any chores I could imagine needed completing, even picking up the office supplies I'd listed out on Friday. Briefly I considered that it might tempt fate to act like I'd already passed the background check which I figured was Stuart's reason for delaying my start until Tuesday, but then I threw a box of brightly colored giant paper clips in my basket and decided I really didn't have much of a background to check. If I wasn't aware of having underworld connections, I bet that Stuart wouldn't discover any. The Slovakian contortionists were Curly's unsavory connections, not mine. Stuart and Derek Irons could discover I was naive and stupid, but not in cahoots with mysterious international figures.

I was ready for work. I went back to the library and looked into private investigators there, mostly so that I'd have to turn off my cell phone and stop listening anxiously for a call from Stuart canceling my employment. The reference librarian, whose daughter went to junior prom with Jeff, helped me find some information on the Derek Irons Agency. She guided me to an online list of private investigator firms licensed in the state. There was a surprisingly well-designed website, including a map of its location. I lost myself for an hour in learning what I could. It looked, actually, pretty boring.

Becky stopped by late in the afternoon after I'd returned home. She brought me a chunky gold-toned brooch that she insisted LOOKED like it concealed a hidden camera, and could probably be fitted for one.

I reminded her I was a receptionist, and we laughed. I'd forgotten to turn my cell phone back on until Becky arrived, and when I did, a beep notified me that a message had been logged onto my account. A text message. I'm pretty bad with text messages. Cell phones have numeric keypads, which are for numbers. The new ones with little bitty keyboards are sized for three-year-old fingers and therefore don't count. And smart phones - well, they just had too much beyond simple phone calling, so I'd been avoiding getting one. That plugged in, I didn't want to be.

It was a message from Stuart.

"It's a message from Stuart!" I announced to Becky.

"What does it say?"

"It's a text message," I said, uncertainly. "So I can't really tell."

"Read it out loud and it might make more sense," Becky advised.

"C u n the a m," it said. I read it out loud. "'See you en the A M'," I read. I was relieved that it translated into English, and relieved by the message itself. It was like a code.

"I hate text messages," I mentioned to Becky between smiling and accepting her congratulations at the confirmation of my new employment.

"Now about those leather pants…" Becky started up again. It took an hour, but I successfully deflected her urgings. I didn't think anyplace had leather pants that actually came with elastic inserts in the waistband, and, after all, I relied on those after a really good day -- or a really bad day -- and a visit to Sweet Melissa's.

Chapter 10

I BECOME INDISPENSABLE

Stuart was ready for me at the office when I walked in five minutes before 9 AM. He'd made hot black coffee and had a bag of plain, whole wheat donuts. The donut bag carried the logo of the whole-foods deli down the street (a smiling pale-green androgynous silhouette in a lotus pose), but the coffee was in the pot of a cheerfully sputtering, shining chrome and black appliance centered on the newly cleared top of one of the filing cabinets. Six sturdy white mugs flanked the device, along with the donut bag. Stuart reached for a mug and the pot and poured out coffee so dark and strong that it appeared thick.

"Welcome to your first day." Stuart handed me the cup of coffee and gestured to the reception desk, where napkins and packets of sugar and sweetener and little plastic containers of cream that didn't need to be refrigerated were piled next to the phone. Nothing else had changed since Friday. I hadn't expected anything to be different. He reached for another mug and poured himself a cup of the brew while I examined my coffee.

"My second day, really."

"Ah. A stickler for details."

"You knew that," I responded, arranging the packets on the desk into orderly piles and selecting three sugars.

"I sure did," he agreed, and passed me the open bag of donuts. I accepted one, placed it on a napkin, and added two containers of the probably fake cream to my mug. The coffee remained disturbingly dark. Two more creamers did little to change the color, and, after another one, I gave up. I tasted the coffee, and even with all the doctoring, and then an additional packet of sugar, it was awful. But highly caffeinated. I picked another donut out of the bag and placed it on the napkin with the first one. Two donuts might be enough to keep the coffee from eating through my stomach lining, but limiting myself to one might be dangerous.

While we sipped coffee and nibbled on the donuts, Stuart told me he was working on several cases that involved gathering data and he'd be in the office for the day, doing computer work. He also said he'd made an appointment with Millie, the woman who'd called on Friday, for later in the week. It was a domestic case. She suspected her husband of being unfaithful. I just smiled and nodded, because I'd gathered that already. It didn't take great detective skills; she'd emphatically referred to her husband as a lying, cheating bastard. I promised to try to stay out of Stuart's way and get to the filing.

By one in the afternoon, Stuart had gotten only two phone calls, one from an advertising company who specialized in coupons on the back of grocery store receipts, which Stuart declined to take, and one from his mother, which he accepted. He spent all morning hunched over either his computer or the phone, while I happily sorted papers into the new folders and neatly printed labels to affix to folders, file drawers, and bankers boxes for older files. I was

41

pleased to discover that most of the stacks did have a sort of organization, and my rate of filing increased exponentially as I deciphered Stuart's bizarre system.

"Lunch?" Stuart asked, poking his head out of his inner office.

"Same place?" I asked.

"Okay with you?" Stuart asked.

"What do you want?" To my enthusiastic ear, our staccato questions made us sound like tough members of a PI agency, even if we looked like a couple of high school teachers.

"Same as Friday, a..."

"I remember," I interrupted. "A carrot juice and a Monterey Jack-style soy cheese sandwich with sprouts and mustard on a whole-wheat pita."

"Good job." Stuart raised a sandy eyebrow, obviously surprised.

"Thank you," I preened. And I shouldered my purse and went out to track down a couple of sandwiches.

When I returned with Stuart's pita and a mock-chicken salad made out of tempeh for me, Stuart was on the floor in his knees-by-the-ears pose. He was humming "Happy Birthday" again.

"What are you doing?" I felt I could ask. I'd already been hired, after all.

Stuart continued humming until he'd finished the song, then unfolded, inhaling and exhaling in some complex rhythm that seemed to coordinate with his motions.

He stretched and stood.

"Yoga," he answered.

"Why 'Happy Birthday'?"

Stuart blushed. I was surprised. I didn't think hard-boiled private investigators would blush so easily. Even if they looked like high school math teachers.

"I use it to time the poses. It takes me twenty seconds to sing 'Happy Birthday' and so I repeat it as necessary to get the right time for my stretching." He bit his lip and added, "I didn't know I was loud enough to be heard."

"I just have very good hearing," I assured him, and passed him his sandwich and carrot juice.

While we ate lunch, Stuart remained on the floor in the lotus position. I recognized it from my youth. I remained at the desk in a chair. The walk to get lunch was enough limbering for me. It didn't seem to bother him that I didn't join him. Which was just as well, as I didn't consider it part of my job description. And I was wearing a skirt. And I couldn't do a lotus position, anyway.

"After lunch, you have some more paperwork," originated Stuart.

"More? I finished the federal and state tax withholding forms. Do you have an application form for the agency?"

"This is to register you officially with the state as part of the agency."

"I need to be registered?"

"So you can do some of the tasks that may come up."

"Like what?"

"It's just a formality. Like if you need to get court papers or something, you'll be more official. We'll make you sort of a junior investigator, and you can investigate phone calls and files and things. It'll just be convenient."

"And was this Mr. Irons' idea?"

"Kind of. Um. Not really. More my idea, actually. Most of the ideas are. Mine, that is. Derek Irons doesn't... think... much. About that stuff."

"Oh," I said, pretending to understand. I fantasized that the mysterious Derek looked like Sean Connery in "Dr. No" and was, like James Bond, running around some tropical paradise dodging evil henchmen while chasing down Big Crime. Of course Derek thought, and had ideas, just not about receptionists and other unexciting things. I knew I was knitting fantasies out of dime novels and campy old movies, but Derek The Mystery Man inspired them. Stuart Wilkins did not.

Ha.

After lunch, Stuart took my fingerprints. He told me they were needed for background checks and things. He sounded kind of evasive to me, but I let it slide. The sleaziest characters in my life were a couple of supple blondes from Eastern Europe, and our only connection was deceased. I scrubbed my fingers even though the ink was some high-tech invisible-on-the-fingers miracle. I like tidying things up and completing tasks, and traces of strange substances on my hands just didn't seem right.

Chapter 11

THINGS FALL INTO PLACE

In three weeks the office was labeled and filed and sparkling. Stuart would leave me alone while he went out, presumably to investigate privately, and he taught me simple online searches. The agency subscribed to several specialty databases, and I became pretty good at the more routine queries. After five weeks, I'd taken over most court searches on the computer and was adept at tracking down phone numbers and addresses. I'd begun learning more about social media and how to find people, and what they were doing. I was amazed at how people who tell their employers, insurance companies, and courts that they are too injured to work advertise their athletic activities all over these sites.

And I still hadn't met Derek Irons. Anytime I mentioned "Mr. Irons" -- and I always did so in a very respectful manner -- Stuart laughed. Anytime I asked a direct question about Derek Irons, Stuart evaded. I may work as a receptionist and administrative assistant, but it did not take considerable investigative skills to realize that Derek Irons was in all probability a testosterone-soaked alias for our own Stuart Wilkins. I decided to play with him. I could always plead menopause and hormonal insanity if he got upset.

"Is Mr. Irons going to be in the office today?" I would ask each morning. Stuart always looked at me strangely, and I would always smile with sweet innocence. Sometimes he just shook his head in the negative. Other times he made up elaborate stories. He could smile with sweet innocence, too. I didn't think I was fooling him. It felt like a game of chicken, only without any real risks. I had taken a physical education course in fencing in college and enjoyed it immensely, even joining the fencing team. My verbal sparring with Stuart reminded me of fencing, and I felt sharp and alert as we maneuvered around the question of Derek Irons. I just liked to keep myself amused, especially since the bulk of the backlogged filing was finished.

Chapter 12

IT'S ALL FUN AND GAMES...

On Tuesday morning of my seventh week, Stuart walked me to the window overlooking the front of the building. Several pedestrians moved on the sidewalk, and he indicated a man across the street.

"Look at him," Stuart demanded.

I did. He was dark, olive-skinned, with dark shaggy hair and a baseball cap. He looked perhaps forty years old, had a mustache, no glasses, and wore jeans and a red tee shirt, both dirty, both baggy. His build was muscular, with a budding gut that looked firm, like he meant it, not like it was a byproduct of soft living. He carried a dirt-smeared tan canvas bag, bulging like it carried tools.

"Stop looking now," demanded Stuart, about thirty seconds later. I did. I closed my eyes.

"You can look at me," said Stuart, "just not at the man outside."

I opened my eyes and looked at Stuart. I raised an eyebrow. Once again, I briefly entertained some doubts about working for Derek Irons, PI and crazy Stuart.

"What did you see?" asked Stuart.

"A hardworking man carrying tools," I answered.

"No, you're drawing conclusions. I want to know what did you really SEE."

"A dirty guy carrying a bag of tools."

"Did you see the tools?"

"No."

"Then how do you know it was a bag of tools?"

"My older son's roommate's father ran a construction firm. He had a bag like that for when he did contractor work directly or helped out his guys. Curly and I got to know Jim and his wife..."

"OK. What did you see?" interrupted Stuart. He was starting to piss me off. I decided to let him have it and answer his question. In full.

"I saw a man, middle height – under six feet tall, I think – with a burly build, a bit of a gut, a red shirt and jeans. He wore a dark baseball cap with shaggy dark hair showing underneath it. No glasses. He had a mustache and was carrying a tan canvas bag with bulges."

"Good." Stuart nodded and made a face like he was impressed.

"And I know he had a left ear when he walked by, because I saw it. But I don't know if he had a right ear." I smirked at Stuart.

"You're right," said Stuart, not at all startled. "If you don't see it, you shouldn't surmise it."

After that, Stuart used to practice this with me before lunch whenever we were both in the office and free. I liked the game, and tried to sharpen my observations to include any distinguishing marks, minor defects of clothing, and odd hitches in the person's movements. Stuart started picking dogs sometimes, and even squirrels. He tried pigeons, but after a few times where I couldn't tell which pigeon he was indicating, he stopped working with them. We both figured that it was unlikely either of us would have to identify fugitive birds. Stuart shortened the time he gave me for observation, and even started trying to distract me.

Chapter 13

...UNTIL SOMEONE GETS HURT

After ten weeks, I still hadn't gotten Stuart to admit anything about Derek Irons, and every time I asked about him, Stuart brushed me off with a laugh. The sparring was fun, but I was starting to feel a bit of a fool and I wanted to be trusted with all the dark secrets of the Derek Irons Agency. I'd filed payroll, and there wasn't anything for a Derek Irons. No tax files, no personnel papers, no nothing. It was time, I decided, to let Stuart know I wasn't a fool.

When I cornered Stuart, one Friday morning, I wasn't surprised with what I discovered – or, rather, what he finally admitted.

"Where is Mr. Irons today?" I asked, as usual, and pretended innocence, again as usual. I thought I'd have a little fun with Stuart and end this charade before it got even more stale. I may be of mature years, but that doesn't mean I'm mature in all my habits.

"He's... out," said Stuart.

"Out where this time?" Once again, I was all innocence, all the way through.

"Special project." Stuart wouldn't look at me.

"Actually, I wanted to ask because there was an important call for him. It sounded very mysterious."

"Oh." Stuart sounded non-committal. I thought fast, trying to remember all the nuances of the plan I'd concocted in the bathtub last night.

"She wouldn't leave her name, but said he'd understand when I said 'On the yacht that Tuesday, the man with the eye patch.' Then she made a comment about a Yorkie and a case of orange blossom lotion. I asked her to repeat it, because I wasn't sure I caught it, and she laughed and hung up. We really ought to look into some advanced caller ID program, you know. This call just showed up as from a restricted number." I sniffed and looked as matronly as possible, which I could do without much effort. I expected Stuart to shrivel under my withering gaze, but he is stronger than he initially appears.

"OK. I'll pass it along when I talk to Irons next."

"Why don't we pay him?"

"Excuse me?"

"He's not on the payroll."

"He's on a special payroll plan."

"We don't have any personnel files on him."

"We don't have personnel files."

"Since two weeks after I started, we do," I countered. "Give it up, Stuart – er – Mister Wilkens, sir, there is no Derek Irons except in your Technicolor imagination."

Stuart started laughing. I'd expected "sheepish," or something similar, but I got "raucous." A medium, beige man like Stuart just shouldn't be able to carry off raucous the way he does.

"When did you figure it out?" he queried, when he'd caught his breath.

"When I did the personnel records and dug into the financial files. Even if a partner or owner doesn't take a regular paycheck, he's going to take something. Even if the business isn't doing well, something goes out. And your business is doing just fine, thank you very much, even though I don't see all that many people walk through the door and you spend an awful lot of time just on the computer, which seems odd to someone like me whose experience in private investigation tends to lean heavily on Hollywood and dime store novels. But I digress." At least I realize I digress, I thought, as I took a breath. Stuart was watching me with interest. I continued. "I'd expect something to go to Derek. Expenses, a bonus, something. And the tax files didn't show anyone but you. I just wanted to see how long you'd hold up. Then I got tired of waiting." I smiled smugly. "And I wanted to see what you did," I added.

"Good job. I'm getting you a PI license."

"What?" Now I was nonplussed. I'd wanted Stuart to be nonplussed by my investigative powers. Instead, he got to me.

"You have some skill at the drudgery of investigation. You need to be licensed."

"Ridiculous," I stated, rolled my eyes, and went to make coffee. It had become my self-appointed task since I choked down the tarry brew that Stuart had made on my first official day.

I do not make coffee well, but Stuart claims he is unable to do better than he did on my first day, and so he lets me practice because, between the two of us, I'm the more likely to eventually learn to make coffee that doesn't drive away clients. My coffee is strong (but not as strong as Stuart's) and I keep the pot full, if not always fresh. Stuart assures me it is already "genuine private investigator style coffee" which means, to him, a fairly efficient caffeine delivery system and not much more.

I brought two cups of my specialty hot, strong (but not as strong as Stuart's), and terrible (but not as terrible as Stuart's) coffee over to the boss. The one and only boss. He was in his dimly lit inner office, once again hunched over his computer. His machine looks like he could run a moon landing from it, in contrast to the simple system on my receptionist's desk. After laying a paper napkin on his desk, I placed Stuart's coffee mug on it and gave him an announcement. I was determined to come up with something to surprise him back. This had struck me as reasonable and fun while I was in the bathtub last night. But the water was cooling, and I was uncomfortable and got out before I'd completely thought this through.

"My next investigation will be into why you never indulge in animal products. Black coffee, soy cheese, no milk chocolate and no pizza, not even vegetarian." I set his coffee down on his desk, near his right hand. "And the investigation following that will be why you work your computer mouse with your left hand at least half the time and you write with your right hand."

Stuart looked up. "Thank you for the coffee," he responded. His eyes gradually cleared and he joined me in the room. When he is deep into an investigation, he seems almost to go into an out-of-body experience and close off. He certainly doesn't always stay in the modest surrounds of the Derek Irons PI Agency. I think of it as Stuart going "into the zone," wherever that is.

"And I'll find out, you know," I assured him.

"Find out what?" Stuart blinked away the last of his fogginess.

"Why you don't eat any animal products, and why you use your computer mouse in either hand."

"Oh." Stuart looked into his coffee cup. I suspect sometimes he's checking to see if there's anything awful floating in it. He doesn't add anything to it, and he knows by now that the cups are always clean when I'm in charge of them. All I can imagine is that he's checking the coffee quality, which is, unfortunately, pretty consistent, but not usually lumpy. Or maybe he's just avoiding me right now.

"You know," Stuart continued, after taking a cautious sip of the coffee, "you are remarkable. The threat of your coffee probably keeps people from coming in and hanging around wasting our valuable time chatting. Yet I'm beginning to actually enjoy the taste."

"Thanks," I said, trying to drip sarcasm. It was obviously lost on Stuart.

"You could just ask me, you know," he added.

I've been getting accustomed to Stuart, and I knew he had returned to discussing my upcoming investigations into his behavior and eating habits. Our growing ability to read each other's minds is scarier than my coffee.

"So why?" I asked.

"It's always better to approach an investigation in the simplest way possible," Stuart began his lecture. "Your question may or may not be answered at all, or it may be answered with a lie or a guess, but you may hit it right there and be done. A lot of people hire us just to find out simple information that's pretty easily available. They just don't know where or how to look or don't have the courage to look."

"Thank you, oh Investigative Oracle," I said. "So why does Stuart Wilkens eschew animal products in his comestibles?" I decided to pester him by going against the simplicity he was recommending. At least in my choice of words.

"Dammit, Hetta, stop talking like you have a British public school education," Stuart said, without heat. "I have a horrifying and rare allergy to certain animal proteins. Or maybe an ethical problem with factory farms for livestock. Now it's up to you to decide which is right or if I'm lying about both."

"And to find out why you use your computer mouse in either hand."

"Persistence is good."

"Required."

"Good, too."

"Good, too," I agreed. "Why do you use your computer mouse in either hand?"

"Persistence," Stuart granted me.

"Why?" I demanded, refusing to be pushed off track again. We were verbally fencing again. I'd never been particularly good at fencing, but I'd been bold, which had been enough to win against my fellow beginners. Talking with Stuart, I really needed to be good, too.

"To keep in practice with both hands. I am ambidextrous in some areas, which can be useful. So passing the mouse around is good practice. And if I use it with my left hand, it frees up my right hand for taking notes. That's all."

"I'll accept that. The animal products one, I'll follow up on a bit. Check into PETA memberships, what you order in restaurants, what magazines you read, and even any articles you may have published."

"Good." Stuart sipped his coffee again. "You could also see if the deli where we get lunch even carries any animal products. It could simply be a matter of convenience and opportunity."

"Thanks, Boss," I answered. "Is it?" I asked.

Stuart just grinned. "I *like* my coffee black," he responded. "Even if it's really, really bad coffee."

"I'll buy you dinner Thursday, Boss," I said. "Sylvio's Steak House?"

"Clever," acknowledged Stuart. "I'm busy Thursday." He grinned at me. "And now," he continued, "we're going to practice observing."

Stuart directed me to the window. This time I correctly observed that the woman APPEARED to be young.

"She has a…"

"'She'?" questioned Stuart.

"I am quite certain that particular humanoid uses 'she' as a personal descriptive pronoun. 'She' does not have even a hint of an Adam's apple. Plus she has a bodacious rack, which is on display."

"'Bodacious'?"

"Yes, 'bodacious.' In this case, I believe it is an accurate and objective description without a trace of subjectivity."

"Oh, really?" Stuart looked like he was about to protest.

"Yes." I was ready for a fight. I reached for my ever-present dictionary on my desk behind us and flipped several pages.

"'Bodacious,'" I read aloud, enunciating carefully, "'Definition 2: remarkable, outstanding: a bodacious story.' Those," I nodded out the window, "qualify."

At that point, Stuart ended the lesson with a bemused nod and a glazed look in his eye. I was pretty sure there was a *touché* in there somewhere.

Chapter 14

I ATTEMPT TO SLEUTH

The next day, I brought in a plate of tiny pastries from a high-end European bakery that was known for wedding cakes. They were working to establish a clientele that would purchase more often than just for their wedding(s) and showcased a different type of pastry each week with a sign explaining its origin. This week, they were pushing Vienna bread, as done in Denmark. The sign explained that we call these treats "Danish" although they were imported from Austria. I chose pastries filled with fruit, creamy sweet cheese, or a combination. I decided I'd watch what Stuart chose to discover just how vegan he really was.

Unfortunately for my investigations that day, five dark-suited men breezed into the front office mere moments after the coffee finished brewing. One of them was Mitch. At least he looked like the Mitch from Sweet Melissa's. Only in a suit, and very well-groomed. And without ice cream. I'd only seen him the one time, and it had been dusk, and he had been attractively tousled. This young man was attractively well-groomed.

"May I help you?" I offered, somewhat surprised at the number but managing to look my unruffled best.

"Here-to-see-Mr.-Wilkens," announced the tallest of the men, somewhat breathlessly. He was gazing at my pastries, which were artfully arranged with tiny clusters of green and purple grapes.

I recognized the longing in his eyes. It was the same look the neighborhood 10-year-olds gave me when I baked cookies in the summer with my kitchen windows open.

The plate of pastries nestled next to the coffee pot. The coffee was undoubtedly too strong, slightly too bitter and with an undertone of burnt toast, but it still smelled delicious. Coffee usually does. Combined with the golden and jewel colored tidbits, it made a compelling presentation.

"We have a meeting here," added the maybe-Mitch. Then he winked at me, and I knew he was definitely-Mitch. "I'm bringing these gentlemen to the office to meet with Stuart, Hetta."

I smiled at Mitch. He was welcome to the pastries. He was my personal angel, like in the women's magazines. I realized I'd never written him a proper thank-you note for the job contact. The thought made me blush brighter than my husband's death scenario. I decided to write the note immediately. While they were eating the pastries and drinking my crappy coffee.

Stuart bounded from his office. "Gentlemen," he nodded to Mitch and the others. "I'm glad you could all meet today."

"Sorry for the short notice," apologized Mitch. "But it looks like you were prepared." He nodded to the lovely coffee tray.

"Hetta keeps everything ready," smiled Stuart. They all turned to me and some of them nodded in acknowledgement. The tall man nodded at the inviting display of pastries instead of at me. I don't think he did that on purpose. Mitch smiled broadly at me, and I blushed again.

Within seconds, Stuart whisked away the visitors (who I later found out were from an insurance company, and were going over a complicated fraud case involving tens of millions of dollars and a prominent clinic), Mitch, all six coffee mugs, the coffee pot, the neatly stacked cloth napkins which I'd brought from home, and the entire plate of pastries. As Stuart returned the now-empty coffee pot to its perch, he smiled and asked me to make another pot of coffee.

"And thanks for being so well prepared," Stuart said, closing the door to his office. As if I'd known about the meeting. I was left with no coffee mugs and no breakfast goodies, not even a lone grape. I glared at the door and decided, if I got really desperate, I'd drink straight from the pot. I wasn't ever that desperate for any coffee I've made. I decided I'd handle Stuart later. (And I tried. I re-used the coffee grounds for the second pot of coffee every day for the next week. It hurt my feelings that he didn't seem to notice. The Food Fanatic columnist in the Hartford Courant newspaper had proclaimed using coffee grounds again was a sure way to make beastly coffee. It hurt my pride, just a little, that I couldn't tell the difference, either.)

An hour later, four contented-looking men in dark suits ambled out of Stuart's Inner Sanctum, followed by Stuart and Mitch. The biggest one, the one who had eyed the pastries lustfully on the way into the meeting, took a route around my desk. He was apparently avoiding any contact with the coffee machine, which he glanced at almost fearfully as he passed by it. I wasn't sure if it was the meeting or the pastries that had them looking so satisfied, but I was pretty certain it wasn't the coffee.

Stuart ushered the four out the door with a pleasant smile. Mitch lingered to give Stuart a thumbs-up sign. Then he came to my desk.

"You are a wonder. The place looks great and it's doing great, too. Thanks, Hetta. I'll keep watching for you at Sweet Melissa's."

I was too dumbfounded to respond with more than a mumbled "Thanks" before Mitch hustled out the door to catch up with the other four.

When Stuart turned to me, his smile broadened to a grin that I think showed his wisdom teeth.

"Derek Irons, Inc has just closed the biggest, baddest contract to date, and we are celebrating!"

"What?" I answered, sounding, even to myself, like I was three steps behind and never catching up.

"Mitch is my front man when I need one. He's good with people. And we are now in the big leagues of PI work."

"What?" I responded unimaginatively. "Is Derek Irons really Mitch?"

"Let me catch you up," Stuart said. "While we celebrate!"

"With pastries?" I was trying to be snotty because I felt ridiculous and left out, but really I'm too old for snotty.

"What would you like?" Stuart offered, undaunted. "We now have an insurance fraud case that'll bring our gross earnings to last year's level within weeks. You're going to learn some tricks on the computer, Hetta my friend, and we're going to have a great time as the fraud-fightin' fearsome foursome!"

"'Fearsome foursome'?" I queried.

"Each of us and our computers," Stuart explained.

"What about Mitch?"

"He'll show up once in a while. When we need his special skill set."

"Special skill set?"

"He looks right. He negotiates. And he put up the initial investment for this agency. He sort of IS Derek Irons, sometimes, only he has a different name."

Chapter 15

MY SLEUTHING IS FOILED

An hour later we were sitting in the waiting area of the office. Actually, it was a corner with three chairs, a coffee table, and a small variety of untouched magazines. I could almost, but not quite, rearrange the magazines on the coffee table while sitting at my desk. Stuart had ordered a large amount of Chinese take-out, and was happily poking a pair of chopsticks into a cardboard container of tofu and dried string beans. I had a shrimp eggroll and chicken with mixed vegetables. And a fork. Containers of vegetarian dumplings and sesame noodles waited on the coffee table.

"Mitch is an old friend of the woman who owns the Pilates studio under my apartment. She introduced us. She's an attorney, but she opened the studio for her niece who had a bit of trouble with an old boyfriend and needed a job in this area. I own the building now and she financed the purchase. She's kind of like a theater angel, but not in the theater. Just in regular life."

I was pretty confused trying to follow this at the same time as I was chasing a sliver of water chestnut around my cardboard container. But I felt relieved that Mitch appeared to be a mere human, albeit a gorgeous and charming one.

"How were the pastries?" I asked innocently, deciding to change the topic. I couldn't think of anything to say about Mitch and Pilates and attorneys without revealing that I hadn't completely followed Stuart.

"Never got a pastry," grinned Stuart. "I didn't stand a chance. Those insurance guys are ruthless with bakery products. Got three grapes, though."

Foiled. Just one cheese Danish and I'd have blasted the vegan cover.

Chapter 16

MY CAREER BEGINS TO CHANGE

That afternoon, Stuart started handing me forms and lists of requirements. He talked about changing my job title at the office to "Administrative Investigator," although I'd pretty much be doing what I'd been doing before. I was reading over the state requirements for becoming a licensed private investigator and realized I'd have to put in a few years working full-time as an investigator. I could cut that time by a year if I took some classes. I considered it and drew out a matrix of pluses and minuses on a yellow pad. I'd been hired for 9 am until 3 pm daily, with a lot of latitude for changes, so scheduling classes wouldn't be a problem. I had the time. I'd taken to staying until 5 or later. I liked the office, it was getting into shape, and I was learning some tricks on computer searches from Stuart. And the house wasn't getting dirty enough to clean all the time. And Becky's joke that I'm likely to continue my home renovations by painting the bathroom red and installing disco lights if I have too much time on my hands sounded just a little too possible. And there was nothing and no one waiting for me at home. I had the time for a class. And financing a class wouldn't be a problem. But I didn't think I wanted to do whatever it was Stuart did all the time.

"Hetta! Come in here for a minute!" Stuart interrupted my musings. I straightened the papers I'd been reading and went in to look over his shoulder. His hair was messed up where he'd been combing his fingers through it, a sure sign he was hunting. And that he was finding something.

"The social websites can tell you a lot." Stuart pointed to the screen, where a photo of a twenty-something year old in a tight miniskirt attempting fellatio on a peeled banana told me more than I wanted to know. "It's amazing what people will share with others."

"Even bananas," I quipped.

Stuart pointedly ignored me and clicked onto a link.

"Now we have a date of birth, assuming he told the truth."

I nodded silently.

"So we'll cross-check it with the posts Banana-Lovin' Girl made to him on and around that day, then see if we can find a criminal record."

"This seems pretty easy," I commented.

"Amazingly so," Stuart agreed, eyes scanning the messages on the screen.

I looked at the screen. "Ewww," I said. Banana-Lovin' Girl had expanded her repertoire. Stuart clicked and changed screens.

"Ewww, again," I said.

"Don't be so queasy," said Stuart. "Or else go get coffee for both of us."

I got coffee. I didn't want to know what Banana-Lovin' Girl would do with an eggplant.

In two weeks, I was doing routine background checks without Stuart checking up on any but the most complicated. I hadn't signed up for a class yet.

"I guess I'm Derek Irons now, too," I suggested one afternoon as I handed Stuart a complete, organized and (I'm sure) flawless report on my latest assignment, a routine background check. Stuart just gave me a look like I had horrifying grooming habits (which I don't) and picked up the report. I guess we don't joke about Derek Irons, the icon. Whoever he is at any given time.

Chapter 17

A BIG CHANGE

"Now," Stuart began one Monday morning, "I have a dilemma and you are the solution."

"Huh?" I hadn't made coffee yet.

"I am swamped with that insurance fraud case this week. And there's a little surveillance matter that needs some attention. Remember Millie, who called one of your first days here, and her 'cheating, philandering, lying BASTARD of a husband'?" Stuart imitated Millie quite well.

"Of course," I answered.

"I think you're ready to move on to the next step of PI work," offered Stuart, obviously trying to sound like I'd just won the Miss Universe tiara.

I wasn't buying it. "You mean sit in a boring car for hours waiting for something to happen? Nope. I'm not physically equipped to pee into a bottle."

"Look, I know it's not glamorous," Stuart began, ignoring my feeble attempts at vulgar humor, or my vulgar attempts at feeble humor. He saw my raised eyebrow and continued, "or even anything other than painfully boring. But that's the next logical step for you to take."

"I'm a receptionist," I stated firmly. "With a glorified title. And sometimes I use the computer for hunting data. I do not sit in cars for long periods of time. And I do not shoot a gun. I am afraid of doing that."

Stuart smiled weakly and sighed. "Someday," he said. "But for now, anyway, let's go over the searches we need to do." He gave me a long list of questions, most of which had incomplete or uncertain data attached to them. Stuart and I spent fifteen minutes going over each item so that I knew what he wanted. I then brewed coffee, poured us each a cup, and added cream and sugar to mine. At last, prepared to find social media posts of workers' compensation beneficiaries hiking, biking and hang gliding, I parked myself in front of my computer and logged on.

By lunchtime, my eyes were crossing and I'd lost faith in the human species. Tracking down people claiming back injuries who were repairing roofs or playing tennis just put me in a bad mood and I was ready for a sandwich, even if it was from Stuart's favorite nuts-and-berries vegetarian deli. I stretched and looked for Stuart to ask him what he'd like me to get for him.

Just then a giant shadow appeared on the other side of the frosted glass door. The distorted shadow had enormous shoulders. For a fraction of a second, I wished I had a gun permit, some training, and a Glock in my desk drawer. Then the door swung open and the broad-shouldered monster became a lanky teen carrying two delivery bags. Stuart popped out of his office, opening his wallet.

I smelled fries. And grilled beef. With cheese. The bags had grease stains. There wasn't a sign of a logo of smiling people in yoga poses, or even grouchy people in yoga poses. This delivery was definitely not from the Healthy Belly Deli. Stuart exchanged some bills for the bags and a big grin from Delivery Guy. He carried the greasier bag over to me.

"Cheeseburger and fries?" Stuart asked, holding the bag out to me. "There's a root beer in here for you, too." He set the less-greasy bag on my desk and fished out two bottled sodas. And a bag of mixed nuts, which he kept, along with one of the sodas.

The bag smelled too wonderful for me to question him until I had cleared off the side of my desk for us (I'm no Stuart, I only had to move two manila folders), arranged napkins and my lunch, and was three bites into the cheeseburger.

"You're not looking horrified by my gluttony," I began, patting my mouth daintily.

"Why would I be?" Stuart asked, popping a hazelnut into his mouth and crunching.

"Meat, cheese, fries…" I gestured at my lunch. "Versus nuts and berries."

"I thought you'd like a break from tofu salad. And I'm softening you up." Stuart scrubbed at his hair until some of the wisps stood on end. He looked like a baby bird, large eyes wide.

"For what?" I narrowed my eyes and vowed to myself not to soften.

Stuart blinked. "I'm stuck. I found where Millie's 'lying, cheating, BASTARD of a husband' is going to be tomorrow afternoon with his lady friend, or at least the motel where he has been going, and I also found a high-stakes golf game where I need to video one of the insurance scammers. I can't do both." Stuart looked worried. He blinked again slowly, twice, his face the picture of woe. "I've been working on finding the motel for Millie for weeks, and now I've got one of the front desk people helping me and we've finally got a lead. But we can't let the insurance company down - I'll have to tell Millie we can't help her…" Stuart looked at an almond with a mournful expression. "She's so upset with her husband's… unfaithful behavior." Stuart, ever the soul of delicacy, didn't look at me, didn't hint in any way that he knew about Curly. I knew he did. Everyone did. It was in the papers. The Circus of the Moon had seen to it that the media covered the contortionists' connection to the show, and that they were innocent of murder, and that they were not after the successful executive's fortune - in short, covering as many of the newsworthy points of harm, money, sex, villainy and fame as possible in order to get their show more media coverage. Stuart knew.

And he got to me. That baby bird look, the reference to unfaithful husbands and wives made foolish by them -- Stuart got to me.

"I'll get the photos for Millie," I said. "She shouldn't have to suffer longer than absolutely necessary."

"Thank you, from me and from poor Millie," said Stuart. His appearance changed, right before my eyes. Stuart's mournful stare became piercing and his narrow face became sharp. He still looked like a young bird. A raptor.

We finished lunch in silence. After I gestured to my remaining fries, offering them to Stuart, and he declined, I swept them and the wrappings into one of the bags and crushed it into a small ball before tossing it in the wastebasket near the coffee maker. I tidied up any imaginary crumbs and smears with a homemade cleansing wipe, and then carefully wiped my hands. A dash of hand lotion from my desk drawer, and I was ready to go over my assignment.

Stuart had been watching me, apparently fascinated, as I handled these housekeeping duties. When I sat down again, he shook himself slightly and took another sip of his root beer.

"So," he began, "you'll be using the camera with the highest zoom lens as I don't want you getting too close. It'll be daylight, and you're not experienced at being inconspicuous."

I nodded.

"The motel is laid out pretty well for our purposes." Stuart pulled a sheet of paper from my printer/copier and, with a few deft strokes, showed the layout of the building and parking area. "You'll park here," he pointed to the edge of the lot. "You'll sit in the passenger seat and pretend to nap. You're looking for a tan sedan, marker number WYM JA5, driven by a medium height, medium build, brown-haired man who looks about 55 and is a bit soft around the middle. I'll show you a photo that Millie gave us." Stuart jotted down the license plate number. "Take a lot of photos of him going into the room. Make sure he's identifiable. Get the room number in at least one of the shots. Take photos of anyone else who goes into the room, and especially of him with anyone else. I've got the date and time set on the camera so you shouldn't have to worry about that unless you fumble around or do something by accident." Stuart gestured at some of the buttons on the camera. "You'll be saving Millie's future, remember that." He looked at me and I wondered why I ever thought he looked like a cute little bird.

He did not.

Another fifteen minutes, and Stuart had filled in the details and given me a laundry list of instructions. I was to drive my little nondescript sedan and not the red Mustang. This is how to use the camera (point and shoot -- I hope I remember). Setting the time and date stamp on the camera just in case. How to change the batteries. Take three spare batteries, all fully charged, just in case (How long does Stuart think I'm going to park outside this motel, anyway?).

Finally, he let me get back to the list of relatively simple data searches I'd begun in the morning. They were tedious, but by the time he was ready to pack up the office, I had a neatly organized report of the data I'd found and was prepared to continue in the morning where I'd left off. If I kept busy, I thought, I wouldn't have time to worry too much about my first real PI assignment. Maybe I should've taken a class. But I didn't want to encourage Stuart. I wasn't at all sure I wanted to be a private investigator.

Chapter 18

STUNG BY A YELLOW JACKET

I shouldn't have worried. Ever. Because worrying didn't make anything go smoother, as the universe pointed out to me once again. All my worrying did me no good, no good at all.

After a morning finishing up the data queries for Stuart, I packed up my little sedan with the camera, some hard candies and a trashy magazine. I put on huge sunglasses and a tacky pink baseball cap with rhinestones spelling out "Las Vega$" which I'd picked up at a second-hand store. I'd laundered the cap in hot water (because I'm afraid of cooties), losing a few rhinestones in the process. I was ready. Stuart checked my understanding of the assignment again, briefly. He agreed I was all set, and he rushed out to the golf course and his assignment. I locked the office, putting up the sign instructing anyone who wanted to see us to call our office phone, and left.

On the way out of the building, I stopped by the restroom. Knowing that I'd be stuck in a car for over an hour made my bladder, normally more of a strong, silent type, suddenly turn whiny and fearful. Two blocks down the road, I decided to stop at a fast-food restaurant to use the bathroom. Just in case. Of course, I had to purchase something. I bought a coffee, and then realized I didn't dare drink it. It smelled heavenly. I knew it would be torture to have it in the car with me, so I poured it into a storm drain in the parking lot. One of the counter workers, the young woman who had served me, was taking a smoke break and saw me. She squinted and her eyebrow rings twinkled. They were very shiny.

"What's the matter with the coffee?" she asked, sounding a little belligerent. Guiltily, I looked up and smiled. I was glad I was already in my sunglasses-and-horrible-hat disguise. I figured she was defensive about her coffee serving skills and I'd offended her.

"Ah just realized ah can't have cawffee this late in the day-uh," I responded, trying to sound like Becky at her most Southern. I hoped that the woman didn't remember my very different accent from earlier. "And it smells so mag-ni-fi-cent that Ah'd be tempted to cheat and Ah'd be up all night." I smiled in what I hoped was an ingratiating manner.

The woman just rolled her eyes and took a final puff on her cigarette. "Whatever," she shrugged and crushed the butt beneath her sneaker before going back inside.

I carefully folded the cup so it didn't leak on my hands and put it in my litter bag in the car. Taking a deep breath, I realized I wanted to pee again. But I decided to remain firm with my bladder, and drove to the motel. I still had plenty of time, assuming Stuart's timetable was accurate.

The motel was unimaginatively named The Luv Inn. I was glad Curly hadn't been found in The Luv Inn. It was humiliating enough that he'd been found in an expensive and elegant hotel. I parked as Stuart had instructed me and clambered rather awkwardly over the center console and into the passenger seat. I didn't want to show myself more than necessary. I double-checked the camera and placed it conveniently. I leaned the seat back slightly and pretended to be waiting for someone, again just in case a Luv Inn employee was watching me. Between looking around the parking lot, I checked my watch and frowned. Any watchers would know that my expected paramour was late.

Apparently no one was suspicious, because an hour later no one had come out of the office. No one had gone into the office, either. I texted Stuart.

"How long do I wait? Nothing yet."

I waited 20 minutes until he finally responded. "Wait until dark."

Was he giving me a movie suggestion? That was not a big help. Ever polite, I answered, "Thnx." Too bad there isn't a font indicating sarcasm. That I know of. Hadn't Stuart told me this would take about an hour?

I settled back and wished for the coffee I'd dumped earlier. At last, a big silver car drove into the parking lot. I sat up slightly and reached for the camera. The Lincoln Town Car had seen better days. The passenger side had a few dents and one of the rear taillights was taped over with red tape, a quick and cheap fix. The license plate was not the one I was looking for, but I was still prepared for Millie's "lying bastard of a husband" to emerge when the car parked toward the end of the lot. First a thin woman in high-heeled sandals and a miniskirt that looked like a tube top doing double duty came out of the passenger side. She wore a short fuzzy yellow jacket and her shiny black hair hung long and straight the way inexpensive hairpieces do. She turned toward me and I snapped several photos. Her yellow jacket was held together by two metal fasteners that left a little gap, showing she wasn't wearing anything underneath. Unless it matched her skin tone. Stuart's drilling on observation had stuck.

Then the driver's door opened and a very tall, very thin, and very young man unfolded from the driver's seat. He wore a baseball cap backwards and grinned nervously at the woman. He looked around and moved like he'd had an espresso or two at lunch. Even though he didn't match the description I'd been given, I snapped a few photos as the woman put a hand on his arm and smiled at him. I wanted to feel I was doing something. To my surprise, the young man must have noticed me. He threw off the woman's arm and dove back into the car. She turned to me and our eyes met. She wasn't pleased. The silver Lincoln Town Car roared into life, jerked backwards and roared out of the parking lot, leaving the angry and almost-naked woman behind. The angry and almost-naked woman who was storming toward me with almost as much energy as the Lincoln Town Car had used in escaping the parking lot.

I tried to put the key into the ignition, but my hands were shaking and I kept missing. I didn't think she had a gun or anything. I didn't see a gun and it looked like there was no good place to conceal one. But she did look pretty fierce, and a lot older and more experienced than her companion. In fact, she looked like she'd ignored sunscreen as a teenager. And in the 30-plus years since. I made sure the doors were locked and the windows rolled up as she bore down on me.

She tapped on my window. I shook my head. She nodded and tapped again, harder. I shook my head again. This time, she showed me a huge metal dome ring on her right pointer finger and indicated, quite clearly, that she was going to break my window. I rolled it down, just a little.

"What do you think you are doing?" she snarled. Her teeth showed some neglect that went beyond missing a day or two of flossing. Then she added some expletives and called me a word that I don't say, even when I've been drinking wine with Becky.

"I'm - I'm sorry," I stammered. "I'm just trying to do my job."

"And just what do you think your job is? He's got to learn to be a man someday, and he's overdue. You can't keep him a baby

74

forever. Do ya want him to live in your basement forever, you -" and she added more vulgarities. She obviously thought I was connected to the young man.

"I'm not here for you! I'm here for someone else..."

"And you took photos of us. Why? For a Disney contest?"

"No, it's my first time doing this -"

"It was going to be Junior's first time, too!" she screamed.

"And I'm sorry he got spooked and ran!" I screamed back, starting to panic and wishing someone would come out of the motel office and get this woman away from me. I began trying to poke the key into the ignition again and, hands still shaking, fumbled and dropped it to the floor.

"Hey," the woman's anger vanished. "You're not Junior's mother, are you? Or even one of her friends?" She looked at me suspiciously. "He thinks you're his mother's best friend in a cheesy disguise."

"I don't know 'Junior' or his mother," I said, grabbing the opportunity to be more angry than the woman. "Who do you think you are, trying to intimidate me? I'm a -" I caught myself before saying I was a private investigator. I didn't know how she'd feel about that. "I'm looking for a lying, cheating snake of a worthless bastard and I'm going to nail his ass." I was snarling. I felt powerfully stupid, acting tough in a pink hat with rhinestones.

Surprisingly, the hooker laughed. "I know a lot of them," she said. "Professional hazard. Looking for any particular lyin' snake?" Her face softened and relaxed, and I saw a flash of someone who I could tell about Curly and the contortionists without feeling like I'd done something wrong and somehow it was my fault that he'd been in a hotel with them.

"How come you're not mad at me anymore?" I asked, my turn to be suspicious, but mostly I wanted to talk with someone who'd blame Curly for being a lying cheater and not me for being inadequate.

"Because you're not a cop or Junior's mom with a gun. Because I've already been paid and I didn't have to pretend that Junior was the best thing I've ever had." She kept laughing. "My acting skills get stretched sometimes. Now my biggest problem is that he'll come back and demand a refund." She smirked. "Not too likely."

"Uh… good," I said.

"So, try to stay away from me, OK? Maybe next time I won't get paid up front." Yellow Jacket started to walk away. Well, sort of sashay away, actually.

I rolled down the window and called out.

"Wait!" I said. "Maybe you can help me."

Yellow Jacket turned around and arched an eyebrow high into her leathery forehead. She walked back to my car.

"I didn't take you as being someone who likes women," she said, almost purring. "But I can certainly accommodate you."

"No! I mean, I'm not asking for that kind of help," I tried to explain. "I'm looking for information."

"Oh, yeah, about any 'lyin' bastard' in particular?"

"Yes. He looks like this." I rummaged in the file I had between the seats and pulled out a photo. I held it out the window. Yellow Jacket snatched it from my hand.

"He looks a lot like Benjamin Franklin, doesn't he?" she mused.

It took me a minute.

"I think more like Alexander Hamilton," I suggested.

Yellow Jacket shrugged and started to hand the photo back to me.

"I meant Andrew Jackson," I amended.

Yellow Jacket snuffled in a way that clearly indicated displeasure.

"Silly me," I said. "I don't have any pictures of Benjamin Franklin, but I do have photos of the Jackson triplets... all named Andrew."

"That would help," agreed Yellow Jacket, studying the photo. "You know, I usually get a tip after a... job... and Junior took off without tipping me."

I dug into my pocketbook and pulled out three twenty-dollar bills. I folded them unevenly so that it was clear there were three and held them out the window. Yellow Jacket grabbed them and they magically disappeared someplace into the skimpy black mini skirt. She then thrust the photo into the car window.

"Nope," she said, and spun away from me.

"Aw, come on," I coaxed. "I saw you recognize this slimeball." Yellow Jacket kept walking. "I have those photos," I called out, inspired.

Yellow Jacket whirled and strode back to me. "Is that a threat?" she growled, bringing her face to my open window.

"Not at all," I smiled, hand on the window control. I was ready to close the window, dive for my car key and get out of there fast, if I needed to escape.

"Look, OK, he and some blonde bitch used to come out here. I've kept that end room for a year, and I saw them sometimes during the day for a couple of months. About three, four months ago I stopped seeing them. I think they went someplace else."

I thanked Yellow Jacket, who then walked toward the street. I didn't want to confide in her anymore about Curly and the contortionists. I just wanted to go home and have a bath. After texting Stuart that I was done and finding my car key, I went home. I stopped for a take-out coffee and a bathroom break after about five minutes. In the bathroom, behind closed doors, I cried until my eyes felt like boiled onions and my head was stuffed up. Meeting Yellow Jacket and my pathetic hope that I could talk with her about Curly had sent my emotions spiraling downward. When I came out,

I made sure my sunglasses covered my eyes so that both I and my emotional state were unrecognizable. I bought an order of fish and chips to go with my take-out coffee, hoping the problem was low blood sugar instead of lingering sadness and feelings of low self-worth.

Maybe I should get a dog.

Chapter 19

SILLY ME

The next day, I told Stuart what I'd found. I also gave him a typed report. I'd left out some of the particulars, like being threatened by Yellow Jacket and bribing her. And my pathetic hope that she'd be a soul sister of some sort.

Stuart's no fool. His work is noticing things and he's very good at it.

"What happened, Hetta?" he asked gently.

I began fiddling with the coffee pot, which was busily brewing the first pot and didn't need attention. But it gave me an excuse to turn my back to Stuart.

"Nothing," I said, sounding as casual as possible. Which meant I sounded fake. Even I could tell.

"Look," Stuart said. "We don't always work with people who are at their best. We meet people who are doing bad things, or stupid things, or people who are hurt by the ones doing those things.

But we get to help make it right. We help clarify the situation. But sometimes it's hard on us. You did a good job yesterday…"

Stuart droned on, soothingly. I wanted to tell him Yellow Jacket had made a fool out of me, just like Curly had made a fool of me, but I just couldn't.

"…and you found information that will help Millie. Let me tell you what is happening with her. Get your coffee and let's sit down." Stuart motioned to the reasonably-comfy chairs in what served as our waiting area.

I nodded and poured cream in my coffee. After taking a sip, I decided it was a four-sugar day. I finished doctoring it and stirring it and out of habit poured a cup, black, for Stuart. Carrying the mugs and a couple of napkins, I walked carefully to the seating area. I was afraid I'd break down if I caught a sympathetic look from Stuart, so I didn't look at him when I handed him his coffee and settled myself. He sat down across from me.

"Now," he began, "Millie and her husband, whose name is Fred, owned a dry-cleaning business. Millie worked there as a bookkeeper and kept the books for three other small businesses, too. Fred sold the dry-cleaning business without telling her. That was legal, technically, because it was in his name. But she thinks he's been seeing someone on the side, and plans to take the money and run away with this other woman. Millie's been finding odd clues to this infidelity and decided to contact us. She's pretty angry with her husband and doesn't want to save the marriage, but she definitely wants to save whatever financial security she has." Stuart paused, then added, "We're not charging her very much."

I knew we weren't. I kept the accounts. We weren't charging her anything, and I never asked Stuart why. That wasn't my job. I also knew that we received occasional payments from a mysterious source that Stuart merely noted as "from the big guy" on deposit slips. I wondered about it and suspected Mitch, but figured that was also not my job, either. I wondered if the mysterious "big guy" was funding Millie's case.

I followed Stuart's tale, grateful he was ignoring my upset. Of course he knew about Curly's death and the circumstances surrounding it. Everyone did. But thanks to Stuart, I was slowly getting pulled back out of my own husband troubles and into Millie's. After all, my lying, cheating BASTARD of a husband had the good grace to die and leave me financially comfortable, if humiliated. Millie's hadn't.

Stuart brought me up-to-date on how he'd found the motel that Fred had appeared to be using, and where I'd met Yellow Jacket. He told me what Millie suspected of Fred and what Stuart suspected Millie was merely imagining. My information from Yellow Jacket had to be considered unreliable, but it was the closest thing to a documented Fred-and-Floozy sighting we had. He was giving me a detailed synopsis and I was carefully following his line of reasoning and how he'd tracked the elusive Floozy so far. By the time he was done, I felt less like a failure, and Stuart's final comment put a smile on my face.

"Your handling of 'Yellow Jacket' was inspired. Getting her help to I.D. Fred on your very first case..."

I beamed. Unfortunately, Stuart continued.

"...of course, you left out how much you paid her for the information. Take it out of petty cash. It couldn't have been that much."

"Thanks," I said. I wasn't beaming anymore. I was busted. I paid a hooker. How embarrassing.

"Quick thinking like that, when you were only expected to snag a couple of photos," Stuart shook his head. "Amazing. On your first case."

"And my last case," I piped up.

Stuart looked me in the eye, all seriousness.

"That would be a waste," he said.

81

I took a sip of my coffee and hoped its heat would account for my flushed face. "We'll see," I told him, while thinking there was no way I was going on another stakeout.

Silly me.

Chapter 20

THE DOCTOR OF

RENAISSANCE MEDICINE

Two days later, Stuart greeted me first thing in the morning with a slip of paper with a name written on it in Stuart's most careful print.

"This is a priority. The books can wait. Bills can wait. Filing, dusting, making coffee can wait. We need to know about this guy's work, any habits and interests we can find, connections. He's applying for a position with a lot of responsibility, and we've been contracted to dig up any dirt. You go onto social media. Check out all his friends, all the contacts you can find. Get me a detailed report, today."

"What's this guy trying to do? Must be quite some job..." I hinted for more information. Stuart knows I'm curious and I think he likes to bait me sometimes.

"It's a biggie," Stuart agreed. "And our work on this is completely confidential. Remember that thing you signed your first week? This is the reason you had to sign it. Sometimes we get work that needs to be kept off the radar - way, way off."

He was grinning. I don't <u>think</u> that sometimes Stuart likes to bait me, I <u>know</u> he does. So I pretended not to care. Sometimes that works.

"OK," I said, noncommittally, and put the slip of paper under a green and blue glass paperweight on my desk.

"Well?" asked Stuart.

"I'll get right on it," I said, taking my eyes off my computer screen and looking up at him. I sighed elaborately as Stuart stayed near my desk. "Anything else, Boss?"

"Frankly, I was expecting some curiosity. You don't recognize the name? Nothing seems familiar to you?"

"No," I responded. "Should it?"

"Yes. You obviously aren't spending enough time on gossip pages."

"I don't go there," I responded as dryly as possible. I haven't wanted to enjoy others' trials and tribulations since Curly's death and the subsequent media attention. I glared at Stuart and tried to set my face into a pose that conveyed "openly resentful" as loudly as possible. I think he picked it up just fine. Because he explained without me doing more than scowling.

"He's dating the daughter of a Fortune 500 CEO. She's about to graduate from a certain local prestigious and famous university, and this young man's doing post-doctoral research there, teaching a class on medicine in the Renaissance. Which class, by the way, is quite popular because the young gentleman oozes enough charm to keep the class full and with a waiting list. And enough charm to terrify the young lady's father. The father, by the way, is paying us a bucket of money to check into the young gentleman." Stuart smiled meekly. "And I know you'll be a huge help in getting this figured out."

"Thank you for the informational peace offering. I will get lunch today," I said, not smiling but not scowling, either. "And poke around on social media sites." I looked at Stuart very directly and very forcefully. "And I will find anything there is to find," I added.

Gavin Taylor, the young man I was investigating, was certainly good-looking in his photo on the university website. Sandy-brown hair, waving slightly, caressed his forehead. A light golden tan and wide smile set off his perfect teeth. I could imagine charm, easily. I scoured other sites. He wasn't easy to find, in spite of what I thought would be an uncommon first name (who knew "Gavin" was so popular?).

True to my promise, I ran out to pick up lunch after almost four hours of almost fruitless searching. It was raining, so I treated myself to the local health food deli's idea of a decadent dessert: organic dried cherries coated with dark-to-bitterness organic chocolate. It went well with my horrible coffee and I even shared with Stuart. It seemed like a good way to seal our peacemaking.

After an afternoon of still almost fruitless searching for dirt on Gavin the Gorgeous, I went over what I'd found with Stuart.

"He plays the zither, and is apparently pretty good. He teaches a couple of classes, which are surprisingly well-attended in spite of the topics being pretty specialized. 'Early Dentistry' was one of them. I have more places to look, but pretty much all I've been getting on him is from his girlfriend's Twitter and Facebook accounts. Luckily she's all over."

Stuart nodded. "Keep it up. I want any photos of him with another woman, or acting up, or anything that is even mildly dusty, if you can't find any real dirt."

I smiled at Stuart. "The loveliest part of this job," I said, and began packing up to go home.

"You're leaving?" Stuart asked, looking astonished.

"Yes," I answered, returning his astonished look. "Gavin may well slip up tonight, and I won't find that out until tomorrow." After all, I thought, it was well past my usual quitting time.

And I had just enough time to run over to the certain prestigious and local university and check in on Gavin's last class.

Chapter 21

UNDERCOVER

Looking like one of the administrators in my plain khaki slacks, conservative sweater, and scarf, I strode purposefully across the campus. I liked to imagine my scarf was jauntily draped and I exuded nonchalance as I waved breezily to anyone who looked official. I'd found class schedules and a map online, so I knew where I was heading and didn't give myself away by looking uncertain. When I reached the correct building I timed my entry so that I went in with a group of people. That way I didn't have to pretend I couldn't find the key pass this prestigious and local university required for most of its building entries.

And I hadn't even told Stuart I was going undercover because I'd been afraid I'd fail. Ha!

I glanced around for numbers, pretending I was searching for a person. Which I was, in a way. Gavin. Inside his classroom, number 4. After I got my bearings, it was easy to find the packed auditorium-style classroom. I slipped into the back. Amazingly, there was an empty seat. Gavin's magnetism apparently pulled the co-eds to the front seats; usually empty spaces were near the professor. I settled in to observe the remainder of the lecture.

He certainly was mesmerizing. Gavin's open face showed an innocent enthusiasm for his topic (which was something about the contribution of common vitamin deficiencies to the diseases of the time). It was easy to understand why I hadn't found anything discreditable on him. He seemed entirely lacking in guile. I'd discovered he'd grown up on a farm in the Midwest, had been a brilliant student and shy with others at school. Late in maturing physically, he'd avoided sports and had worked on his studies and his family's farm, which primarily grew soybeans. He'd picked up the zither in college and became quite adept based on a couple of reviews of amateur concerts. I'd learned the zither is most commonly used simply. To attain Gavin's level of playing required some dedication.

I was probably getting a bit of a crush on Gavin myself. Maybe it was just a result of being surrounded by his adoring students. All that adoration rubbed off. But I sort of wanted to adopt him and feed him cookies. He appeared to be the human equivalent of a Golden Retriever. A particularly smart, talented and well-groomed Golden Retriever.

The course period ended and the students reluctantly rose from their seats. Several went to the front of the room to ask questions. Gavin listened attentively and responded to each in turn. A couple of them moved close to him, touching his arm and smiling up at him. Gavin remained polite and focused on the questions. He ignored the subtle flirting. After thoughtfully answering a question on vitamin D, Gavin glanced up toward the door by where I was standing. His face lit up. I started to automatically smile back before I realized his attention was on the door. When I turned I saw a young woman entering the room. Her face glowed and her eyes were locked onto Gavin. She was Jaci, the Fortune 500 CEO's daughter. I recognized her from the photos I'd seen earlier.

Gavin made his excuses to the students still surrounding him and went to Jaci, taking her hands and smiling down at her. I couldn't quite hear what they said to each other, but he draped an arm around her shoulders as they went back to the podium at the front of the room. Gavin gathered his notes into a canvas messenger bag and they left the room, still murmuring to each other. And still aglow, both of them.

I knew there would be no dirt on Gavin. I knew they were in love. Or at least infatuated, I thought bitterly. It was impossible not to think of my early days with Curly, when I thought we were destined for each other and the future seemed ripe with possibilities. But I couldn't remember a time when his face had glowed like that when he saw me. Maybe I'd just forgotten. Maybe the memories were crowded out by my imagined images of him dead in the hotel room with the twin contortionists.

I went home and scrubbed all three bathrooms, even washing the walls hard enough in the blue bathroom that I thought I might have to repaint it soon. After I finished and the bathrooms gleamed and my hair smelled of bleach and lemons, I peeled off the rubber gloves, made a cup of tea, and sat down at the computer to write my report on Gavin. I left a place to add anything else I found tomorrow, but I was sure there would be nothing discreditable. I'd just seen Romeo and Juliet without the complication of warring families. And I wanted to go for ice cream therapy at Sweet Melissa's.

Which I did.

Chapter 22

A TASTE OF SUCCESS

Murriel and George were out at a family function of some type, the teen at the counter wasn't sure what they were celebrating. They did have both mocha chip and the new starry night ice cream flavors, and Mitch didn't appear to be among the patrons. While sitting outside with a small starry night cone, I scanned the crowd. Maybe Mitch would materialize and bring some sort of wisdom or solution to my restlessness.

The ice cream therapy wasn't working, so I walked back to my car, throwing out the uneaten part of my cone. When I got home, I put my rubber gloves back on and scrubbed the kitchen. And then, I could sleep.

The next day, I found that Gavin and Jaci had gone to a birthday party for Gavin's mother. Jaci posted a couple of photos. Everyone looked happy.

I found no dirt on Gavin. Or Jaci. I forwarded my report to Stuart electronically.

"Sorry," I said, bringing coffee into Stuart's office. "I found nothing even remotely incriminating on Gavin Taylor."

Stuart looked up from his computer screen and smiled at me. "I didn't really think you would. And don't be sorry. In investigations, the best thing is to find something. The next best thing is to find out that there is nothing to find. And it's not good at all to find something that isn't there."

I'd included in the report that I'd gone to Gavin's lecture and seen him with Jaci, even mentioning my impressions as objectively as possible. I included a photo of the two of them together that I'd taken surreptitiously while pretending to check my phone. Stuart pulled the report up on his screen and scanned it while I stood there, cradling my mug of coffee.

"This is quite good. You did a thorough job and sitting in on the class was a good idea. Your report covers it all. Nice, Hetta, really nice." Stuart smiled up at me. "Along with what I found - or didn't find - we'll have an encouraging report to give to Jaci's father. Assuming he likes Gavin, anyway."

I felt quite pleased with myself and looked forward to my next foray beyond filing and bookkeeping and coffee-making. Silly me.

Chapter 23

STUART SIDELINED

"Hetta," croaked the voice on the other end of the phone. "It's Stuart."

I wouldn't have recognized his whiskey-and-chocolate voice. He sounded like a cement mixer full of bullfrogs. Irritated bullfrogs with respiratory problems.

"I need your help." Of course he needs my help. That's why I work for him. But he sounded like a man in the final throes of being drawn and quartered, so he probably needed extra help now.

"What can I do for you, Boss?" I asked. "You sound like you're being drawn and quartered," I added, helpfully.

"I have the flu," he explained.

Good. I had hoped he wasn't in the final throes of being gruesomely executed. The flu, I could handle. So long as he didn't want me to do anything too icky. I'd raised my kids, and had decided I'd reached my limit of unwanted body fluids and other nastiness, at least until either Edward or Jeffrey graced me with grandchildren.

"Remember the Robertson case?" the voice creaked.

"Of course," I responded. "The one with the 'lying, cheating, bastard of a husband'. I did that stakeout. It was ten days ago."

"That's the one. I need a stakeout tonight, and I'm running a fever. You'll have to do it."

"Can't it wait until you're better?" I didn't do stakeouts anymore, after that first fiasco. I was a receptionist. And a filer. Sometimes a computer records hunter and gatherer. And a coffee maker, of sorts. But NOT really a private investigator.

"No."

"What?" The voice had just croaked. It had sounded like it said "no" but I didn't want to believe that my mild Stuart would disagree with me. He even drank my coffee.

"NO!" Definitely a loud and negative croak.

"I'll call you right back," I said, and hung up. Maybe this was a prank call and not really Stuart after all.

I dialed Stuart's cell phone.

"Dammit, Hetta," he answered, in the same sort of croak, but unfortunately quite clear. "I need your help to get that nice Millie Robertson's husband nailed so she can take him to the cleaner's in divorce court. I know he's got a date tonight with his floozy, and I need some photos." Stuart's voice lost some of its croaking with use. Or with impatience. I certainly understood him.

I kept track of Millie Robertson and her case since she called the day I'd started at "Derek Irons, PI." Her husband, Fred, had been pretty careful lately, and it had even started to look like the floozy might be a product of Millie's imagination -- and Yellow Jacket's affinity for photos of dead presidents printed in green. Three days ago, Stuart had followed Fred Robertson to a motel, where he had taken a room and then left, alone, about two hours later. Stuart had then spoken with – and very probably bribed – the clerk.   He'd learned that a man matching Mr. Robertson's description (which wasn't difficult to match, but was very difficult to match with certainty – "medium height, graying medium brown hair, medium build") met a blonde woman almost every Monday and Thursday evening.   Looked like Yellow Jacket and Millie the Deceived Wife were right. And this was Thursday.

I weighed the options. We had a lot of work. Putting off until Monday what should be done today wasn't a sensible option, but one I certainly embraced in this case. But Millie's husband was a cheating philanderer, a villain I could really enjoy foiling. I wanted to help her, and Stuart wasn't going to be able to, so it was up to me. And as Millie's phone call was the first I'd taken for Derek Irons, this case was a sentimental favorite. I was going to do this even if I didn't want to, and I was going to end up making the best of it and probably even pretending it was an adventure. And I was going to brag about it in the future. To someone, somewhere. Maybe to my sons, if that wasn't breaking some code of PI honor, and almost certainly to Becky. Maybe even Mitch, if I ran into him at Sweet Melissa's. But I had to do the job before I could plan how to boast about it.

"Of course," I told Stuart, nonchalantly. Had there ever been any doubt that I'd take on this task? "What do I do?"

Stuart gave me the address of the motel. He said I should be there well before dark and find a discreet place to park and watch. He told me where the camera was, and what I'd need. I knew where the camera was. I'd made the place for it. But I didn't annoy him by explaining that. He sounded really awful, awful enough so that I hoped I wouldn't catch the flu from having worked in the same office when he was probably spewing the virus like Mount Vesuvius spewed ashes all over Pompeii. In fact he sounded bad enough that I thought I could probably catch the flu by talking on the phone with him, over the wires, like it was some bizarre mixture of computer and biological virus.

Stuart described in great detail the photographs I needed, the shots we wanted to get but weren't vital, and how best to do this. Angles, light, the camera lag on his digital (none) and whether I could shoot through the car windows (better to have them open, but not an absolute requirement unless they were really dirty). I took notes. He didn't know how long I'd need to wait. He told me to bring paper and a pen to write down anything of interest (I made a notation to bring TWO pens, in case one ran out of ink, because I'm thorough like that). He said I shouldn't fall asleep, or read, or get too distracted, because the photographic opportunity could pass quickly, and my word would not be worth much, but some solid photos of Millie's husband with his floozy were golden. He also reminded me NOT to drive the red Mustang.

Duh.

Stuart went over everything again, varying the order. I didn't know if he was confused by his illness or nervous about me doing the job. Finally, Stuart reminded me again not to drive my red Mustang and told me to call him with any questions. I promised and told him not to worry about a thing and to hurry up and get well.

"Sure," he said, "and be careful."

I laughed and hung up the phone. I wasn't afraid of a cheating husband, especially someone else's.

Chapter 24

I PINCH HIT FOR STUART

After I hung up the phone with Stuart, I took a deep breath and surveyed the room. The office officially closed in half an hour and I could really just put up a sign at any time, which is what Stuart used to do before I came on the scene. Most business was conducted via phone or pre-set appointments, and the answering machine was quite adequate generally for taking calls. I turned it on, and set it so I could hear the calls come in and answer if necessary. Then I pulled a canvas duffel bag out of the closet and started to pack for my evening's adventure.

Maps. Lots of maps. I also packed Stuart's GPS, and I had my new phone, but I really liked maps better. I got the address of the hotel, two photos of Millie's Cheating Husband Fred, Millie's address and phone number just because I thought it was efficient to do that and they were in the same file as Fred's photos, a tripod for the camera (there was room in the bag) two bottles of soda (with caffeine) and a package of sesame and whole grain crackers, which I loved, and two chocolate bars, which I loved more than the crackers, for emergency energy. I packed three CDs (one of The Beehive Queen, one of Patsy Cline, and one of the soundtrack of "Top Gun") in case I needed entertaining or inspiration. I carefully packed the camera and lenses in the camera case, and added that to the duffel bag. I packed night vision goggles, for no particular reason except they are cool and were stored in the closet near the field glasses, which I also took.

And then, fatefully, I poured the half pot of coffee that Stuart hadn't been in to drink into a thermos and slipped it into an outside pocket of the duffle bag. I cleaned the coffee pot, double checked that everything that should be off was off and everything that should be on was on, carefully locked the door, and left to begin what I was considering a big adventure — only because I'd never done real PI stakeout work before, except for the botched incident with Yellow Jacket. I figured before the night was out, I'd be bored enough to consider tackling Stuart's filing system a refreshing and exciting challenge.

Silly me.

Chapter 25

THE WHISPER INN

I went home to change cars, as I'd driven the Mustang that morning. I drove it almost every morning, because I liked the idea of it, and the manual transmission made me feel like a capable professional. I'd even taken to wearing British-made black leather driving gloves with crocheted backs, which I carefully took off and left in the car because, although they made me feel good, I knew that, in reality, driving gloves worn by a slightly plump woman of mature years and conservative driving habits behind the wheel of a bright red Mustang could only attract ridicule. Facing the reality of my PI work, I changed clothes (unfortunately charcoal-colored sweat pants, sneakers, and a navy blue long-sleeved t-shirt instead of black leather pants, boots and a black turtleneck sweater) and cars (into my dark green four-door sedan instead of a silver Aston Martin) and headed for the stake out.

The motel was easy to find. The Whisper Inn advertised its presence, and available vacancy, none too discreetly with a four-colored neon sign and several sporadically blinking lights. Fourteen units faced the road, each door sporting a different combination of base color and trim, and the parking lot had a narrow blacktop strip leading around back to what appeared to be a maintenance area. I parked in a corner of the lot that afforded me a good view of the office door and most of the units. There was a pickup truck next to me, but I backed in and kept my little sedan's nose just far enough out so I could watch without being easily seen.

Five minutes after arranging the car in the parking lot, I'd arranged and re-arranged my stake-out equipment four times, finally to my satisfaction. Three minutes later, I'd nervously downed both chocolate bars. I didn't remember eating them, I just found myself staring at the office door and holding two empty wrappers, with the lingering taste of chocolate on my lips. Trying to calm my nerves by snacking has been a problem for me.

I tried to concentrate on The Whisper Inn's décor and landscaping, such as it was, amusing myself by practicing the observation drill Stuart regularly put me through. After studying the area for 30 seconds, timed on my watch, I closed my eyes and tried to recall details. Without Stuart there to correct me, I had to peek to check my accuracy, but that was fine, since I didn't want to keep my eyes closed for very long in case Philandering Fred or The Floozy showed up. The Whisper Inn, I noted, was covered in white siding made chalky with age. Each door had a unique color scheme, and I suspected that the owner had found a bargain bin of lively enamels at the local paint store. Mauve and lilac, lime and yellow, melon and orange, pink and sky blue, sky blue and orange – the colors competed with the gaudy neon sign for attention. And won, too.

I contemplated the plantings. The Whisper Inn boasted the kind of box hedges that your average Grandma and Grandpa used to keep neatly trimmed to geometric shapes with squared edges and, occasionally and somewhat less successfully, to rounded shapes. These were not trimmed to any sort of geometric shape, or any sort

99

of shape at all. They weren't trimmed, even, but sent spikes shooting in every direction like a teen-ager's weekend morning hairdo. There were flowers scattered among the bushes. A lot of the flowers were the purple heads of clover or orange day lilies gone wild. There was no grass to mow; any place without bushes or flowers was either covered with concrete or worn to the dirt.

Chapter 26

NECESSITY

After fifteen minutes, I felt sleepy. I fished the thermos out of the pocket in the duffel bag and poured my first cup of coffee. That was my first of many mistakes that night. I'm not counting the chocolate bars.

The thermos started out full. It held a quart. My bladder did not. With still about half an hour before I could reasonably expect Millie's Philandering Fred to show up with The Floozy, I began to realize my error. Female private investigators can't urinate into a bottle. Or into a coffee can. I began fantasizing about things a female private investigator COULD urinate into, and the best item I could come up with came under the heading of "modern bathroom facilities." As I had given up thinking of anything other than my increasingly urgent situation, and was beginning to look for any convenient foliage that could pretend to serve as modern bathroom facilities, a car pulled into the parking lot.

It was Philandering Fred's. I recognized the license plate.

That brought my mind back from thinking about the advisability of ducking behind the yew hedge before full dark (I wasn't in quite such dire straits yet). I watched Fred stroll into the office and come out, two short minutes later, swinging a key. He should have looked furtive. I'd have respected him more if he'd appeared to have a conscience. I wanted to run him over with my car, or, better yet, the large and ruggedly used pickup next to my car. But I knew that Millie, with the photos I'd give her, would run him over more effectively and more painfully in divorce court. So I watched as he entered the unit with the mauve door with lilac trim, second from the end nearest my corner. I'd clicked off at least three photos that showed him and the room number on the door as he was unlocking and entering it.

I needed a bathroom, and I just was not going to make do with the ratty foliage around The Whisper Inn. Either I abandon my post (unthinkable!) or find a better solution. I thought hard, and, necessity being the mother of invention and all, decided a real bathroom, with real facilities, was the only real solution. And I was right next to at least fourteen of these, and, from the looks of the parking lot, at least ten were probably still available.

While Philandering Fred hadn't been furtive, I was. I didn't want to run into The Floozy, or miss her, either, so I moved quickly but watchfully. I ducked into the office and asked for the unit with the lime green door and yellow trim. I babbled that those were my favorite colors, because I wanted to make it seem sensible that I would be picky about which of the sad units I was given. The unit with the lime green door and yellow trim was the end unit, next to Fred's, and an easy dash to and from my car. The office manager, a young man with several rings through various parts of his visible anatomy and an almost visible aura of disinterest, handed over a set of keys in exchange for a modest collection of bills and I almost ran to the end unit.

I noticed the curtains by the mauve and lilac door were closed, but dim light peeked out around them. There was a muffled sound of voices and background music and canned laughter. Philandering Fred had the television on.

Some lover, I thought.

But then I decided my qualifications as a critic wouldn't hold up – I'd lost my husband to indiscretions that, perhaps, I could have prevented. I'm sure I could have prevented them, if I'd been a set of extremely flexible Slovakian twins.

I pushed those thoughts into a back compartment of my mind, labeled "Worry About Later" or, possibly more accurately and in the tradition of old mapmakers warning of uncharted and probably dangerous territory, "Here Be Dragons."

As I was completing my transaction with the modern facilities, I heard a woman's voice from next door. The walls were pitifully thin. Her voice, high pitched and sharp as an assassin's dagger, carried easily. His voice remained muffled and both were rendered meaningless by interference from the television. Dammit, The Floozy had arrived while I was otherwise occupied. I'd have to wait for them to leave. I hoped Fred suffered from premature ejaculation and we could get this tryst over with quickly so I could get the photos and go home.

I tried to listen, straining my ears and willing myself to unravel sense from the almost-heard, almost-comprehensible words. Nothing. Four glasses wrapped in paper sat on the vanity next to the sink. I remembered reading that an empty glass, held – somehow – to the wall would amplify sound. I lifted one of the glasses. Not glass, but a disappointingly flimsy plastic. Would plastic work? I held it open side to the wall. It didn't work too well, so I tried closed side to the wall. Past training in high school physics eluded me, so I even tried it sideways. The voices remained incomprehensible. I searched for glass containers. Did I have a glass container in the car? A bottle that I could break? I gave up, and put my ear to the wall, and heard plenty. In fact, I heard much more than I wanted to know.

"…Honeybunch. And we'll get a little place in Tennessee, in the hills, and live off the land." That was Philandering Fred.

"Let's plan tonight, first." The Floozy had a practical side. "You got what you're supposed to do?"

"Yeah, yeah, Cupcake. I got it down. We just gotta keep our eyes on the prize, so we remember we're doing this for us, for our future…"

Doing what? I thought. Old Fred wasn't very enlightening, but this did not sound like foreplay.

"Go over it step by step," demanded The Floozy.

This was good, unless it <u>was</u> foreplay. Then it would probably get icky.

"I go home and bring her a bucket of chicken."

"Bunch of flowers," corrected The Floozy.

"But if the florists are all closed, a bucket of chicken," stated Philandering Fred, hopefully. "Besides, she might get suspicious if I bring flowers."

"You were supposed to check on florists," reprimanded The Floozy, her voice higher.

"I forgot. But Millie likes fried chicken," said Philandering Fred.

"Fine. Go for flowers first." The Floozy sounded grumpy. "Maybe get both. She'll like that. Go on," she prodded.

"And I leave the door unlocked, and go to check it when everything's ready for you to come in," Philandering Fred continued.

"Yes…"

"And then I don't lock the door but I turn the light on, and you come in and finish."

"You'll have to help with that," warned The Floozy.

"I will," said Philandering Fred, hesitantly.

"Of course you will, my big, strong, STUD!" Sounds of wordless murmuring, and I imagined The Floozy was encouraging Philandering Fred. I tried not to imagine exactly how she was encouraging him.

I went as far away from the adjoining wall as I could, which was outside near some of the bushes, and dialed Stuart on my cell phone. He didn't answer. He was probably pickled in some vitamin-soaked health-food-store flu remedy, sound asleep.

What could I do? I'm not a skilled private investigator, or much of a skilled administrative assistant. I'm definitely not skilled in coffee making. My fencing success had been built on being bold. I reverted to boldness and strode into the motel office, fishing in my pocketbook for my lipstick case with the little mirror attached.

"Hell-loo!" I sang out to the empty desk, over the sound of a TV sitcom coming from a room in the back, partially viewable through an open doorway. The lights from the television screen caused a frantic flickering on the battered trim around the doorway.

"Hell-loo!" I repeated.

"I am coming. Please hold on." The raspy voice preceded, barely, a very short woman with a bleached blonde shag haircut and a cane. She brandished the cane without really using it to help her walk. She walked by throwing herself across the room, rocking violently from side to side on twisted, but serviceable legs.

"How can I help you?" she asked.

"What happened to the young man who was here earlier?"

"Raymond is my son. He's in the back." The woman glared at me. "He's cleaning his gun," she said.

"I rented a room from him earlier," I explained. "I found a lipstick holder and wanted to know who the couple next to me is so I could check with them to see if she lost it." The story sounded pretty weak to me, and it didn't look like the short woman was buying into it, either. I pushed the detritus around in my purse. I

105

should have made sure I had the lipstick case in hand before I rushed into the office. Maybe boldness wasn't always the best option.

"Let's see the item," she said, suspicion dripping from every word.

I frantically ran my hand over a pen, my house keys, the office keys, a pack of saltines (crumbled but not yet leaking) from Monday's lunch, and a battery for the penlight I had in my pocket. I'm a neat freak everywhere but in my purse.

"Is there a woman in the unit next to the end one? I think it's number 2." I found a comb, a pack of mints – and a lipstick case.

No response. I held out the lipstick case. "I found it outside the unit's door, and I thought it might be something someone would hate to lose. You know how awful it is to find the perfect shade of lipstick and then not be able to get it again." I hoped she'd warm to me with this shared confidence, woman to woman. I hoped I'd charmed her enough so that she'd give me the woman's name.

No such luck, on any count. The petite purloiner plucked the lipstick, with the clever little case that prevented it from opening in my pocketbook AND included a convenient sliver of a mirror just large enough to reflect a pair of lips. She examined it carefully from all sides. She opened the case and removed the lipstick. She opened the case and twisted the lipstick into view. A coral shaded into tan, conservative, matte, fairly expensive and without a trace of glimmer. The blonde dwarf looked at me and back at the lipstick.

"My son Raymond has already cleaned my gun," she stated, conversationally. "And this lipstick doesn't belong to the woman in unit 2 any more than it belongs to George Washington. What are you trying to pull?"

I needed the name, so I could call the police. Or at least that was my current plan of action. Maybe I should just attack Shorty and grab the records. Maybe I should just break down the door to Philandering Fred and The Floozie's room and stop them, armed only with a plastic cup and well, maybe a tire iron. Or maybe I should just call the police and report all the license plate numbers in the parking lot and what I'd heard.

I reached over and snatched the lipstick from her hands as she was tucking it back into the case. I'm pretty quick and I surprised her. She regained her composure pretty quickly.

"I think you'd better leave the property," suggested the woman.

I turned and left. I dialed the police emergency number on my cell phone.

Chapter 27

MY OWN HANDS

Basically, no one wants to take a middle-aged woman's version of a conversation half-heard through a motel wall very seriously, particularly if the threats were indirect, at best. I wasn't sure which part of the formula made me less believable. In my feminist heart, I hope it wasn't the "middle-aged" or the "woman" part. I was assured a police car would drive by Millie's and Fred's house a few extra times throughout the night. I was not reassured. I gave up and tried Stuart again.

No answer, so I left a voice message. I may have expressed a little frustration.

It was time to take matters into my own hands. The suspicious blonde was peeping out of the office window at my car, and I wondered if she'd send Raymond and The Gun after me or try her luck with the police dispatcher. I was betting on Raymond and The Gun, because Shorty seemed pretty direct. There was still some time; the television's neon flickering still danced on the edges of Fred and the Floozy's window curtains.

I called Millie. No answer there, either, and her answering machine, had a man's voice on it, probably Fred the Philanderer's. I'd have thought that was sad, if I hadn't been wound tighter than one of my Great-Aunt Ethel's pin curls. Even though I talked for a long time – some may even have characterized it as "babbling" – Millie didn't answer. Perhaps she wasn't home, which would be good. Perhaps she was taking a bath, or in the shower, and disturbing images from the movie "Psycho" prodded me into action. There was nothing more to be done, I was going to have to go to Millie's myself and rescue her.

I should have thought of calling Mitch.

But I didn't think of it. Plus, I didn't have his phone number. And I wasn't sure how to spell his frighteningly complicated last name.

Chapter 28

TO THE RESCUE

As a fairly competent and extremely nosy administrative assistant, I had painstakingly filed Millie's address (the competent part) and noted it (the nosy part) and remembered it (again, the nosy part). It took a few minutes for me to orient myself, but I was on my way before the Floozy and the Philanderer turned off the television. If they ever did. But that was another image I didn't want to think about for long.

Millie's home was an easy drive, and traffic was light. I was in front of her house before I'd really figured out what I was going to do. So I fell back on my fencing strategy of 40 years ago: boldness.

There was a light on in the front room. No television flickering that I could see. No porch light shining. I parked a couple doors down — that was a tricky private investigator move in case Fred was clever enough to recognize a familiar nondescript sedan from the motel. Well, I could be careful in some areas, while practicing overall Boldness. I wasn't careful enough to remember to bring my purse in from the car. My purse with my cell phone in it, and my IDs. But I was concentrating on Boldness. And I was terrified.

The porch fairly vibrated with comfort, furnished with two padded wicker chairs, a little wicker table and several pots of blooming flowers placed to provide decoration with a minimum of tripping hazard. It looked like my porch would look, if I had a porch like this one, and decided to furnish it. I admired Millie's wonderful taste in furniture and decorating, briefly, and empathized with her poor choice in men, somewhat less briefly.

The doorbell sang a cheery tune. I waited. Music played inside, and then I heard footsteps. Uneven, uncertain footsteps. The door opened a crack and a single sad eye peered at me.

"Millie?"

"Who wants to know?" Belligerent with bourbon, if my nose was working properly. It was. My eyes were almost watering from the fumes.

"I'm Hetta - Hetta Moon – from the Derek Irons Agency. I'm here because your life may be in danger." Boldness, again.

"Are you a PI?"

"I'm here to help." I put a lot of assurance into this, while slyly avoiding answering. It worked like a Jedi mind trick from the Star Wars movies. Enough boldness on my part, a cloak of self-assurance, and Millie believed that I was capable of helping her. Since she was soaked in bourbon, I figured I didn't really need all that much boldness or assurance. But right now, even without bourbon, I believed it, too. Boldness, indeed.

Millie opened the door to me. I took in the scene: a movie was paused on the television screen, with a comic actress caught in the middle of an evil chuckle. I recognized the movie; she was a spurned wife who exacted vengeance on her ex-husband and his replacement wife. I'd watched it, too, but it wasn't terribly inspirational for me, since my husband was dead and beyond my

111

revenge fantasies. A glass and a bottle of readily affordable bourbon sat on coasters on the coffee table flanked by a box of tissues. A wastebasket next to the table proved that the tissues had been in use, in case Millie's streaked face left any doubts. The rest of the room gleamed, immaculate and orderly. A mauve flowered couch perched between matching end tables that were coordinated with the coffee table and another end table next to the dark blue recliner that was obviously Fred's (although it had doilies on the arms and the back to protect these areas from skin oil and wear, stains spreading from beneath the snowy lace served as evidence of failure. The room was painted ivory with a rosy undertone. A half dozen pillows that looked like they'd been crafted in a series of weekend workshops on home decorating perched plumply on the sofa and chair. A scattering of framed photographs, all of cats and small dogs, decorated various flat surfaces, each marooned on its own little white crocheted doily island. I noticed that Millie had a mauve "princess" phone (which had been my heart's desire as a teenager) standing sleekly on its own doily island on an end table next to the sofa. There weren't any dead leaves on the plants, not even the ficus tree. I marveled at Millie's green thumb, my ficus always sheds leaves. In fact, the leaves on Millie's plants looked polished.

I recognized the symptoms; I shared them.

"What can you do?" queried Millie from behind a tissue she was dabbing against her nose.

"Your husband and his floozy are plotting to kill you. We're going to surprise them. We're going to leave."

"Can I kill him first?" A gleam of life in those sad eyes.

"Not until we can establish self-defense," I replied. "Then, go ahead."

Encouraging Millie may not have been my brightest idea, but she looked so dejected, and that seemed to give her hope.

"He deserves it," Millie assured me.

"I have no doubt. Let's get your shoes on."

112

"I'm not leaving."

"I want to keep you safe."

"I want to shoot Fred." Millie burst out in a sob that grew into a wail.

"I understand. Let's get you out of here."

"I don't feel right!" Continued wail.

"What's wrong?" She didn't look nauseated, but my kids used to wail and say they didn't feel right just before they vomited. I took an involuntary step back.

"I WILL NOT be forced from my home!" Millie shrieked.

"I understand," I assured her. I was relieved about the vomiting. "But you'll be safer at my house."

"No, no, NO!" More shrieking. She sounded like a two year old.

"I have bourbon at my house," I cajoled her. It didn't work. Maybe I should have offered cookies. "And we can make brownies." I sensed a hesitation between the shrieks and the wails, and pressed my advantage. "And have them with ice cream from Sweet Melissa's."

I pushed too far.

"Fred always got me ice cream for my birthday!" and the decibel level increased again.

"Millie," I began to reprimand her, "you don't…"

"YOU don't… YOU don't understand," Millie got very quiet, very suddenly. She pulled herself up, and I realized she's a pretty strong-looking woman. I'd have to rely on coaxing her, not physically overpowering her. "He has been lying and cheating and taking advantage of my good… my good… my good…" Millie was struck with an attack of hiccups and sounded like a stuck record. "Of my kind nature," she completed her thought with dignity and only a minor hiccup. "So I am not leaving my home. Besides," Mille narrowed her eyes, "I'm not leaving MY house so that he can take it over. Tomorrow, I'm getting the locks changed." She shot

113

home the bolt. "I have an appointment," she assured me, with drunken dignity.

I admitted defeat.

"OK, you win. But we have to make you safe. First, let's secure the perimeters." That sounded very competent and professional, I thought.

Millie and I checked every door and every window, together, because I didn't trust her in her current state. I made sure everything was locked. Millie even had nails in the downstairs window sashes. I was impressed. She didn't have an alarm system, but I figured I'd performed that duty. She was warned.

"What next?" asked Millie, eyes now shining, but with plans of violence, not with unshed tears.

"We need supplies," I improvised.

"Like…?"

"Rope, to secure the perps." I sounded tough and professional, at least to myself. "And a couple of kitchen chairs, sturdy, to tie them to. Flashlights, as heavy as you've got. A bat, or a sock with a couple of bars of soap in it, to subdue them as necessary. Phones." I was digging deep, trying to keep us busy. Waiting was a little nerve-racking. Realizing my phone was in my purse in my car was a little nerve-racking, too. I wondered if Fred the Philanderer was going to find flowers or if he'd settle for just fried chicken.

"Let's hide the knives," suggested Millie.

"Good idea," I answered.

Millie pulled a red fake leather shoulder bag out of the front closet and dumped its contents on the closet floor. The little pile contained a surprisingly motley assortment of lipsticks, pens and paper scraps accompanied by a worn wallet and a little cosmetics bag. She left the pile and closed the closet door after pulling something from the closet shelf and dropping it into the bag. Then she moved into the kitchen and emptied the knife block into the bag.

"Do you think I'd cut myself if I put a couple of these in my waistband?" she asked me, brandishing a handful of steak knives.

Since I thought she might hurt herself just touching them, probably would sever an artery if she put them into the bag, and would undoubtedly draw large amounts of blood by tucking them into her waistband, I nodded and suggested she forget about the knives.

"Now we need to set the scene," I suggested. "To trap Fred," I added, and Millie nodded eagerly and continued nodding for a little too long. She was pretty drunk. "Setting the scene" was going to involve coffee and food and trying to sober her up, I thought. There was entirely too much going on just with Millie. Fred and The Floozie's arrival would spin the situation totally out of my control. And I needed to be ready to call 911 immediately. And figure out how to convince them that the situation was genuine.

Millie's cupboards and refrigerator had been organized. Very well organized, like mine. I found everything I wanted quite easily, in spite of Millie's questions about what we could use as weaponry. She really started to get creepy while I made coffee and she rummaged through her kitchen gadgets.

"How about this?" she asked, holding up a pastry brush. We could tickle him on the bottoms of his feet and make him talk."

"Nice," I responded absently.

"Here's something," she crowed, and brandished a vegetable peeler like an epee. "I could gouge out his moles like the eyes in a rotten potato!" She looked at me gravely. "Fred has a lot of moles."

I winced. Involuntarily. At the thought of Fred and his moles as well as what she wanted to do with them.

"Now you KNOW what I could do with this baby!" Millie crowed, this time holding an egg slicer.

I didn't know, and I didn't want to think about it. And I really, really didn't want Millie to describe her ideas. Millie dropped it into her shoulder bag to join the knives, the pastry brush and the vegetable peeler. I grasped Millie's shoulder and moved her to the coffee maker. She needed to be distracted from her bloodthirsty fantasies. This was going to be hard enough without her going even further out of control. I needed to get that bag away from her. It had finally dawned on me that she wasn't really hiding potential weaponry, just making it easily portable.

"Do you have a tape recorder?"

"Huh?" Millie looked up from rummaging through a drawer of implements that were looking increasingly dangerous to me. Millie had opened my eyes to the possibilities for mayhem in an ordinary kitchen. She had the bag slung over her shoulder, keeping it handy so she could slip sharp and pointy things into it. "Why do we need a tape recorder?" she slurred, examining a flour sifter and dropping it to the floor.

"So we can get him to talk and have it recorded."

"Is that legal?" Millie asked.

"It is in this state," I said. I didn't know, but what I did know was that I needed to get her away from that drawer or I'd never be able to cook again without having disturbing images dancing in my head. Millie nodded seriously, once, and wandered upstairs, coming down after just a few minutes with a cassette recorder circa 1980, complete with fresh batteries and a blank tape. The bag still hung heavily from her shoulder. I really needed to get it.

"Milk? Sugar?" I poured two mugs of the strong coffee.

"Definitely something," Millie responded. "It looks like tar," she added, critically. She absently shrugged off the heavy shoulder bag and hung it on the back of a kitchen chair.

"That it does," I agreed, and poured a good dose of cream in her mug, then added three spoons of sugar. Somewhere I'd read that alcohol stole sugar from the body. Or added it. Or something.

I figured nothing could hurt Millie more than Fred had, or was planning to, so I added another spoon of sugar. I treated mine more gently, with half the cream and one sugar, and herded Millie to the sofa. She carefully placed coasters for our coffee mugs.

"Here's the plan," I began.

"This coffee looks pretty bad," originated Millie.

"Yes, it does," I agreed.

"I know what it needs," she added and glanced at the bottle of bourbon.

"No!" was my first response. Then I took a sip of the coffee. It was worse than pretty bad. It was awful. "Well, maybe." She wasn't going to drink it. Another sip. "OK." I figured she wouldn't drink any of it without bribery, and maybe the caffeine would overwhelm a little splash of alcohol. I hoped so, anyway.

Millie poured whiskey into her coffee, filling the mug to the brim. I'd left plenty of room in the mug because I wasn't expecting her hand to be very steady, so she'd added a generous amount of whiskey. She poured some in my mug, too, before I could stop her. It wasn't much more than a splash, because, being sober, I'd left less room in the mug. But she topped my mug off, too. After carefully placing the bottle on a coaster, Millie stared at her coffee mug.

"Oops," she said. "Too full." She slid off the sofa to her knees and bent to sip from the mug without lifting it. She slurped happily, and then looked up. "Not too hot anymore," she explained with a smile.

I watched her for a moment, and then went back to the kitchen. This woman was going to need food. Crackers, cheese, salami, peach yogurt, mixed nuts, Bridge mix, baby carrots and a chocolate bar with nuts and raisins all went onto a tray. I had to dig in Millie's shoulder bag, which she'd left hanging on a chair, to get a knife to slice the cheese and salami. I felt around gingerly, not wanting to find any sharp edges unexpectedly among the disarray. What I did find was a cold, smooth object of disturbing shape and weight. I didn't know calibers, or makes, or models, but even I could recognize a handgun.

Deciding that me, sober, was safer at handling a gun than even an expert (which I doubted Millie was) who was drunk (which I knew beyond a doubt Millie was). I pulled out the gun and tucked in into the back of my pants, like I'd seen tough cops and PIs on television do. I hoped it wouldn't shoot me in the butt. I knew there was a "safety" that could be "on," but had no real idea how to check it. Unless there was a really big button, and it was very well labeled, preferably in primary colors, I wasn't going to figure it out. I did unhook the bag from the back of the chair and wedged it into a little space between the stove and the cabinets.

I brought the tray into the living room. Millie was still kneeling at the coffee table and drinking from her mug. Tears streamed down her face. I placed the food in front of her. I went back to the kitchen and brought the tape recorder into the living room and put it on the sofa under a pillow. I'd turn it on if the opportunity arose to wring a confession from Fred the Philandering Weasel.

"OK, girlfriend, let's finish this movie. We're ready for anything now!" I maintained a cheery attitude, in spite of the cold gun digging into the small of my back. I helped Millie up onto the couch, put the tray of snacks on her lap, and pressed the remote to restart the movie. I began working the gun out of my pants and into the space between the seat cushion and the back of the sofa. I thought it would be safe there, if I made sure it was pointed toward the floor. The gun was almost positioned where I wanted it to be when the movie restarted. It had been stopped mid-cackle, and the raucous sound started me. Luckily my hand was nowhere near the trigger. I patted it into place and leaned back, relieved. Millie never flinched. Good thing, or our snacks would have landed on the floor.

We enjoyed the movie. It made no sense, really. There we were waiting for what I was certain was a plot on Millie's life to unfold, but it seemed unreal. I thought I could keep her safe in her locked home, and we were sisters in the Floozy Follies, and I was starting to really like her, too.

After all the snacks were gone (surprisingly quickly), and I'd sipped on my coffee a bit, just to be companionable and to settle my nerves, I returned to the kitchen and found cherry chocolate chip ice cream and chocolate sauce and even a can of whipped cream which, although not as good as freshly whipped cream, is infinitely better than no whipped cream at all.

I made sundaes, modest ones, with nuts. The second round of sundaes weren't so modest. I drank more coffee because the ice cream made me thirsty. I wasn't sure if Millie had laced it when I wasn't looking or if it was just the remnants of the first cup that flavored my second coffee. But I didn't care too much.

By this time, we were watching the director's cut of the movie, which we agreed was a bit pretentious, because the movie was fluff and we began discussing the merits of movies and what made a movie "fluff" versus "meaningful," and whether "fluff" movies deserved a director's cut. Then we began looking for hidden meaning in the movie, theorizing that any movie with a director's cut must have some, and then I brought the carton of ice cream and the chocolate sauce and the whipped cream and the few leftover mixed nuts into the living room. I was beginning to believe that nothing was going to happen, and I'd imagined the sinister overtones in the overheard conversation.

Then the doorbell rang. I jumped. Millie looked toward the door and grinned. After seeing that grin, I was very, very glad I had the gun tucked away and had hidden the knives.

"It must be Fred," Millie almost purred. "I feel inspired by the movie."

"Act normal!" I instructed.

"Then I'd have to shoot him." Millie rose from the sofa and turned toward where she'd left her bag. "That would be my normal."

"No! Just let him in. Let him talk." I was a professional. "We're going to tape him."

"OK," she agreed with some hesitation. "But if you weren't telling me not to, I'd normally want to shoot him right about now."

"He may be bringing fried chicken," I tried to mollify her.

"I hate the fried chicken he gets. He gets the cheap greasy kind with no spices and I don't think it's cleaned very well because I once found a pinfeather in it, fried right into it, and now I won't eat it. There may be internal organs still hanging onto it, if there are pinfeathers."

"Oh." I didn't want to think any more about Philandering Fred and his fried chicken pinfeathers. It was making me think about Stuart maybe being vegan, and I might understand why. I tried again with Mille. "He might be bringing flowers."

"I hate the flowers he gets. He gets those cheap bouquets with a lot of that stuff that crumbles and drops off really fast. Or else he gets me half-dead roses from the back of a truck. I hate him."

"Me, too," I agreed. "But we still can't shoot him. We'll get him in court."

"Real bad?"

"Real bad," I assured her, without even correcting her grammar. And confusing adjectives and adverbs is a pet peeve of mine. But I excused her because she's drunk, and she has to answer the door and we don't have time for a discussion of grammar. And I was wishing I hadn't had so much ice cream and gotten so thirsty and finished my coffee with bourbon. But I was a professional, and PIs drink all the time. I read it in a book. Never mind that the book is part of a fiction series so soaked in testosterone that the PI is an ex-Navy SEAL named Dirk Derringer. I needed to concentrate. I don't hold my whiskey as well as Dirk Derringer. Who is fictional. Along with his capacity for alcohol.

Millie strode to the door, all determination. I wished I'd checked her for makeshift weapons. I'd read – probably in a Dirk Derringer book – that a ballpoint pen could be used as a weapon. I hoped Millie hadn't read Dirk Derringer.

Millie opened the door.

Chapter 29

FRED THE PHILANDERER

It was a Boy Scout, in uniform, selling wrapping paper to fund a trip to the Boy Scout Jamboree.

"I'll take three packs," said Millie. "Do you have a Boy Scout knife?" I left the couch and rocketed to Millie's side. I was going to need to get this situation back under control. Or under control for the first time.

"Yes," said the Boy Scout, with some hesitation. He wouldn't be trying to strike any flints near Millie's breath.

"Can I buy it?" Millie asked. "I seem to have misplaced my knives. And my gun." I jabbed Millie, discreetly. She grunted, which wasn't very discreet.

The Boy Scout smiled weakly. "I – I don't have it with me," he stuttered a bit. He turned slightly away from the door and began to step backwards.

A figure walked up the driveway.

"He's here!" Millie sang out. "Get the gun!"

"Act natural," I hissed.

"I naturally want to shoot him!"

The Boy Scout had reached the bottom of the steps and turned fully toward Philandering Fred, walking up the driveway with a bucket of fried chicken *and* a bouquet of unidentifiable flowers. Fred had parked on the street in front of the house.

"Hel – hel – hello," the Boy Scout greeted Philandering Fred. The Boy Scout looked like he was still hoping to complete the gift wrap sale.

"Hello, young man," said Fred. "I'm just bringing my lovely wife dinner and flowers to celebrate our many happy years of marriage." He held out the offerings to show them. I could see the bucket of chicken was from "Clucker's," which was known to local teen-aged wags as "Frickin' Chicken" or some even less dignified names. I believed there could be pinfeathers and maybe even internal organs fried into the greasy coating. The flowers were indeed brown-edged white carnations and lots of papery, dried fill surrounding one slightly limp red rose. I was unimpressed, and thought maybe Millie was justified in wanting to shoot him.

The Boy Scout looked at the bucket of chicken. "'Frickin' Chicken'?" he asked.

"Huh?" said Philandering Fred, hesitating briefly as he passed the Boy Scout.

The Boy Scout just watched Fred as he continued up the steps and onto the porch, apparently giving up on selling gift wrap.

"Hello, Dumpling," Fred sang out.

Millie glared at him.

"You're early," she said. "We haven't finished watching the director's cut of the movie yet. You're always early. You're always done when I'm just getting started. Premature."

"Let's all go inside and sort this out," Fred suggested. "With chicken," he cajoled, raising the bucket.

"Get me my gun! Get me a knife!" shouted Millie.

"Go inside the house, NOW!" I demanded. I put a lot of assurance into it, and the Boy Scout, wide-eyed, was the first to move.

"Not you!" I hollered and pointed to the wide-eyed Scout. "YOU GO HOME! We are having what is called a domestic dispute here. I will handle this. Go home!"

"Wrapping paper?" he asked weakly, trying one more time.

"Call the police for me," I hissed. "Get them to come here. And GO HOME! Do it NOW!" I thought maybe the police would listen to a Boy Scout. He turned, glanced backward, and then ran, clutching his bag and a catalog.

"Now YOU," and I turned to Fred, who was almost as wide-eyed as the scurrying Boy Scout. "Inside." I pointed. "You, too," I added to Millie, who was patting her pockets with so much energy it looked like she was committing minor assault on herself.

"NOW!" I roared, and they both flinched and walked through the open door.

Chapter 30

HETTA, HETTA MOON

"Now," I said calmly, "You are going to sit down – not near each other!" I physically pushed Millie away from Fred. "You," I grabbed Fred's arm, still cradling the flowers (I didn't want to get too near the chicken bucket – visions of deep-fried pinfeathers and internal organs were swimming in my head) and shoved him toward the armchair adorned with doilies on the arms and back. "And Millie, you sit on the sofa," I added considerably more gently.

"Who – who are you and what are you doing in my house?" sputtered Fred, trying to play the Indignant and Wounded Husband. That wasn't working on me. I'd seen the crappy chicken and the low-end bouquet. Fred had a lot to answer for.

"The name is Hetta. Hetta Moon." I tried to sound like James Bond, in the more recent movies where the actor said it like it was frightening. Then I realized I should have said "The name is Moon. Hetta Moon." I just needed more practice.

"She's rescuing you from me shooting you, you murdering bastard," spat Millie, sitting obediently on the couch.

"Millie, Peaches, what are you saying?" Fred wrinkled his brow started to stand up.

I growled at him, and he sat back down.

"You lying, cheating, philandering, fornicating son of a diseased – and pockmarked – and mole-covered – BITCH!" growled Millie, who had apparently read some of the higher-browed bodice rippers that decorated the bookshelf.

"Dumpling…" crooned Fred to Millie. He leaned forward, then glanced at me and sat back again.

"I am not your dumpling, or your peaches, or any other of your fruity little nicknames…"

Inspiration hit me like Marla Braeburn's schnauzer hits a sausage dropped on the floor (I've had breakfast with Marla and her schnauzer). Domestic disputes can be called in to the police. The police come for those. They come for any call to 911. A little mayhem in the background, and the place would be covered in blue uniforms within minutes. All I needed to do was…inspire the combatants. I had small hope for the Boy Scout.

"She says you have a little dick," I said to Fred.

"What?!" Fred answered.

"And he doesn't use it very well," added Millie.

"What kind of a husband brings such sorry-ass flowers?" I added some fuel.

"Limp as his dick," said Millie.

"What!?" Fred added a touch of outrage.

"I said, 'Limp as his dick,'" repeated Millie, in a significantly louder voice.

"It wasn't so limp earlier, when I had a real woman." Fred wasn't using cute nicknames any more.

"What?!" I asked.

"What?!" echoed Millie. "You're admitting it, you lame, cheating shadow of a man."

I scrambled to find the tape recorder. I was going to start it. The tape would last for over an hour.

"Yes, and proud of it. I can satisfy a real woman just fine."

A tinkle of glass stopped further discussion of Fred's attributes.

Chapter 31

The Plot Thickens

It was the bourbon bottle. It hit the door, then the stone flooring in front of the door.

"Look what you made me do!" Millie roared her displeasure. "I wasted the rest of the whiskey! And it's you and your little dick's fault!"

I reached for the phone on the end table near my end of the sofa. Three decorative and plump pillows acted as a barricade, so I stretched to reach. I felt a little light-headed – no doubt from the excitement and adrenaline. It was time for action. This was sounding like a domestic dispute. All I had to do was pick up the phone and press three digits – the police, I knew from TV shows, would trace the address and rush to the scene. I'd be over and done with this. I knocked the phone off the cradle but before I could punch any buttons, Millie was on me.

"Kill him for me! You're a cop, so kill him, it's legal for you," she demanded, and tried to shake my shoulders. "You'd be defending my life. He's gonna make me puke to death!"

Fred rolled his eyes dramatically.

Then I heard the back door handle jiggle. I knew it was locked, so I started to peel Millie off me and reach for the phone to punch in those three magic numbers before Fred the Philanderer could cross the room and stop me. Glass tinkled in the kitchen as the back door window broke and shards landed softly on linoleum. My hearing, jacked up and waiting for this, picked up the noise each sliver made.

"Oh, damn!" I heard from the back. The sound wafted through the open window. Fred turned as if cued. He probably was. Millie stopped begging me to use my non-existent police powers and looked toward the kitchen.

"What's that?" Fred the Philanderer said, as though reading from a script. Pause for several beats. The back door handle jiggled. "I'll go see what's happening!" he intoned. Definitely scripted, I thought.

"I'll call 9-1-1!" I announced.

"No!" said Fred, and changed course abruptly. "I'll handle this!" He jerked the phone away from me and jerked several more times until the cord, jammed behind the sofa, loosened up enough to be pulled from the wall. "Oops," he announced, "look what I've done. I don't know my own strength." He glared at Millie. "As Man Of The House, I'll protect us from any Unexpected Intruders."

I hadn't often heard people speak in capital letters, but Fred the Philanderer, and two of the kids who had been in Edward's third grade play, were able to pull it off.

Fred strode into the kitchen, looking as manly as someone with no chin clutching a pink Princess phone could. Or at least making an attempt at it.

"What Are You Doing Here?" intoned Fred, opening the back door. Then, quietly, "you were supposed to break in yourself!"

"Look, Dumbass, the window left glass on the edges and I didn't want to cut myself. It'd leave DNA evidence," the Unexpected Intruder hissed. "Is she tied up yet?"

"No, because I was outnumbered - there's another one here!" whispered Fred, The Man Of The House. He wasn't as quiet as he thought he was, or my hearing was better than he'd expected, because I heard him quite clearly.

"Find another phone and dial 9-1-1," I instructed Millie, slowly and carefully and much more quietly than Fred's hiss. "NOW!" I added somewhat more sharply and pushed her away from me as I rose to go to the kitchen.

"Look, you couple of dumbasses…" I walked into the kitchen and stopped in front of the gun. Blondie the Floozy had a steady hand. I don't know much about handguns, or calibers, but this looked big. Much later, Stuart explained to me that most guns look big from that angle. The angle where it's pointing at you and you can see the hole where the bullet comes out.

"Shut. Up." Blondie was dressed in black. Tight black, with a black bandanna accent covering the lower part of her face and another one almost covering her hair. Bits of blond cotton candy-like fluff stuck out around her ears. "This is a robbery, and I don't want anything to go wrong so someone would get hurt."

"Please Don't Hurt My Wife." Fred pleaded unconvincingly. "I'll Give You Whatever You Want."

Millie surged into the room.

"Done!" she called out to me. "So this is your floozy?" Millie turned to Blondie, ignoring the gun still trained on my nose.

"What do you see in him?" Millie asked. The gun moved halfway between Millie and me.

Blondie the Floozy growled. "Hand over your valuables!" she said, trying to disguise her voice with a pitifully inadequate accent that I thought might be an attempt at New Jersey. The gun zeroed in on me again. "Or I'll shoot this bitch." I stopped thinking about her accent.

"You count Fred as one of the valuables? I'll pack his suitcase. Whether or not you shoot her." Millie spoke very loudly, and sounded very drunk. "She's my cousin's wife. There's no insurance, she's just a pain in the ass," Millie ad-libbed.

I would have been offended, but I was concentrating on the gun. The muzzle looked huge. It was that angle thing.

"Cash! Jewelry!"

"You think that skinflint got me any jewelry?" Millie almost shouted, and laughed derisively. "He's never even gotten me a decent bucket of fried chicken. He goes to 'Friggin' Chicken,' for Pete's sake. You're not here to rob me! You want to kill me for the insurance that my stupid husband said he'd get on me. Which he didn't, by the way. I handle the checkbook."

"Friggin' Chicken?" The gun waivered.

"Yeah, and check out those pathetic flowers!" Millie gestured to the sad little bouquet on the table. "Brown-edge carnations, a limp rose and cheap filler."

"Those are the flowers he got you?" The gun waved toward the bouquet.

"Yeah. What's he ever gotten you?"

"A big old diamond necklace." Blondie was bragging.

"Yeah? Diamond?" Millie raised an eyebrow. "Do you think anybody living in this little house is buying a big old diamond necklace for anybody else?" Millie gestured around the modest room.

Blondie looked around. The gun lowered. "He said it was a diamond."

"How big?" Millie asked.

Blondie pulled a necklace out from under her black t-shirt. A large diamond solitaire hung on the fine silvery chain. "Two and a half carats," Blondie said.

131

"Two and a half carats of glass, hanging on sterling silver, I'll bet."

"Platinum," said Blondie, glancing at Philandering Fred, who was looking less "Man Of The House" and more "Chicken Little" by the second.

"See if it's showing any tarnish. I'll lay you five-to-one odds it's tarnishing right now."

Blondie looked down, snorted and jerked it off her neck, snapping the chain. "What IS this piece of shit?" she roared at Fred. "PLATINUM... DOESN'T... TARNISH!"

"Buttercup..." Fred began.

"Why don't you call her 'Peaches,' you sniveling sneaky snake?" Millie's voice should have carried to the neighbors' houses, easily. I listened for police sirens. Nothing yet.

"Sweetums..." Fred turned to Millie.

"Try scratching something with that sorry piece of fakery. If it's a diamond, it'll scratch glass. Try it on the picture over there." Millie waved her hand to a photo of Fred in front of a car, smiling broadly.

The Floozy rubbed the stone against the glass, and then peered at the glass and the stone carefully. "Nothing," she stated.

"Hmmm," said Millie.

"Hmmm," I echoed.

"I can explain!" said Fred.

"I hope so," said the Floozy, and this time she was glaring at Fred. The gun, forgotten, was pointing at the floor.

"How much life insurance did he say I had?" Millie queried the Floozy.

"Two million dollars." The Floozy looked like she was doing some calculating, and it might be giving her a migraine.

"I have enough life insurance for a little funeral, a really little one with a really cheap casket. Want to see the papers? I'm very organized," Millie offered.

"Fred, if you've been fucking with me…" warned the Floozy, and the gun was covering him now.

"Baby Sweet, we'd have the house and everything…"

"You can have the house as long as you take Fred, too, and with my blessing. He farts at the dinner table, you know," Millie added. "Plus, we have a mortgage."

"I should shoot him for the fake diamond."

"You should," Millie agreed. "A woman gives the best years of her life, and what happens? She gets fake jewelry and false promises." Millie burst into tears.

I was hoping to hear police sirens, and soon.

Chapter 32

COMPLICATIONS

The Floozy looked at Millie.

"Do her now!" screamed Fred. "And her too!" He pointed at me.

"You FART at the dinner table?" asked the Floozy.

"Shoot them! I mean, Don't Shoot! I'll Fight to Protect My Home!" Fred added, as an afterthought, "and My Family!"

"Oh cut the crap, Fred." The Floozy walked over to him and nonchalantly hit him on the head with the gun. Fred crumpled to the floor. The Floozy tossed the gun onto the table next to the discarded necklace, knelt down beside Fred and began checking his pockets.

"Look at this mess!" I decided to try the boldness plan again. "What do you think you're doing?"

"Right now," the Floozy sighed and pushed the bandana back off her forehead. More blond fluff sprang out and formed a lopsided halo around her made-up face, now collapsing into a frown. "I'm re-thinking my options." She knelt next to Fred.

While the Floozy rifled Fred's pockets, I handed Millie tissues and got the clothesline. Millie snuffled her tears back and, the Floozy finding nothing of interest, the three of us wrestled Fred into a chair. I tied his hands behind his back and tied each foot to a chair leg. I was wrapping the rest of the clothesline around his torso when he came out of the fog. He wasn't happy.

"What's going on here? I've been attacked! Where's The Intruder?" Fred stopped when the Floozy stepped in front of him, now without the disguising bandanas, and waved her fingers in his face.

I knotted the end of the rope. There were at least twenty circles around his torso, arms and the back of the chair. I'd put in knots every couple of turns, so that it wouldn't be easy to work loose. The Floozy arranged the bits of booty from Fred's pockets on the end table next to a candy dish: one handkerchief of questionable cleanliness, a set of keys, a wallet with three five-dollar bills sticking part-way out of it, and a pair of corroded nail clippers.

Then, at last, I heard police sirens.

Chapter 33

HELP ARRIVES

Millie and the Floozy, who introduced herself as Joy, went to the front door. They were working out what they wanted to say to the police. I just wanted to tell the truth. Joy wanted to blame Fred for everything. Millie argued every point, on any side, and drunkenly contradicted herself every which way.

Three police cars, lights blazing, parked at angles in the front of the house. Dark figures raced to the back of the house on each side. More sirens sounded, moving closer. A voice called through the bullhorn.

"We have you surrounded. Come out peacefully and no one will get hurt."

I glared at Millie. "Did you hang up the phone after you called the police?"

"Of course not! This way they could trace the address and come over! And they could hear what we said," Millie sniffed. "And everything. I watch television shows. I know this."

I sighed. The police probably thought we had a hostage situation or something. I shouted "I'm coming to the door, it's OK!"

I opened the front door, slowly. "It's OK!" I sang out again. "I'm Hetta Moon, with the Derek Irons PI agency and everything is under control."

Then I noticed that same view again, looking down a gun barrel, only this time it was in plural. At least half a dozen guns pointed at me.

Boldness.

"Guys, it's over. We've got the bad guy tied up." I took three steps onto the porch, legs trembling like half-cooked spaghetti and mouth desert-dry. "All done," I added, as cheerily as the view would permit.

I waved. All the guns stayed in place.

The bullhorn again.

"Come out slowly with your hands up."

I raised my hands. "Come on out, ladies," I called cheerily over my shoulder. I heard a dragging noise from inside the house, and a muffled squealing.

"Out of the way!" cried out Millie.

"Here he comes!" called out Joy.

I stepped away from the doorway as Fred, securely tied in the chair and gagged (I thought I recognized his own questionably clean handkerchief), rolled onto the porch through the front door. Half the gun barrels moved to cover Fred and the kitchen chair. I wondered how they decided who covered what. Was there a class in police school that taught that even-numbered birthdays moved to any new target while odd-numbered birthdays stayed on the original? But then what if there are TWO new targets – or even more? I was babbling, but silently. Probably the result of all those gun barrels.

Or the bourbon-laced coffee and adrenaline.

Joy and Millie peered around each side of the door. Fred, on his side, squealed angrily and rocked the chair.

"Is it safe to come out?" one of them called out. I didn't recognize Millie's voice, so I thought it must be Joy, without the fake accent. I stood still, hands raised, Fred struggling and squawking at my feet.

"Come out slowly with your hands up," repeated the bullhorn.

They did. Millie looked like a movie star walking the red carpet. She gave little waves with her upraised hands. Joy hung her head a little, and I thought she looked sheepish, but then I realized when Fred's squeal changed into a higher pitch that she was just looking for some part of his anatomy to kick. "You used too much rope," she said to me. "He's padded."

I followed Joy down the porch steps. I thought I could keep her from bolting. After all, I work for a private detective agency. She wasn't likely to bolt with five police cars and a mob of cops bristling with weapons, but I wanted to stay focused on my job.

"Millie's safe now," I assured the first cop who I could look in the eye.

"He's bulky. He may have a bomb strapped to him," someone said.

"It's clothesline," I explained. "A lot of it."

"Shoot him and see if he explodes," suggested Millie. She didn't sound like she'd sobered up at all.

"Pat down the women for detonators," someone ordered, and we were patted quite thoroughly, especially Joy. "Keep your hands in the air," commanded the officer patting me down. I did.

Finally, satisfied, someone went to rescue Fred, who was still squealing.

"I'd take the gag off last," advised Millie. The officer ignored her, and Fred began babbling immediately.

"I didn't do a thing, these crazy bitches came after me and I don't know what they had planned – they began talking about my personal attributes and I think they were going to kill me and you've gotta lock them up and throw away the keys because they're menaces…"

The officer looked at Millie again, before tackling the clothesline, and nodded, once, to show she had been right. Then he turned back to the clothesline. When he got close to the end of the unwinding, he motioned for backup. Fred was still complaining. A whiney note had crept into his litany of wrongs. I wanted to kick him, too.

"And there I was, coming home to my little wife with dinner and flowers…"

"A bucket from 'Friggin' Chicken' and brown-edged carnations…" Millie, hands still in the air and waving, added commentary between teeth gritted into a smile.

"Handcuff them all and we'll sort it out later," ordered someone with more decorations on his uniform than the others. "Domestic disturbance, for starters."

I was mortified. Millie was angry. Joy burst into tears. Fred was still complaining. Someone read each of us our rights. The burly officer who told Fred he had "the right to remain silent" added "and it would be very much appreciated."

We were separated from each other. I hoped the other women would remain silent, but I wasn't expecting them to stay quiet. Millie actually growled when she passed Fred. Then Joy did, too. I thought it was good that she'd stopped crying. I clung to my remaining shreds of professionalism and gathered them around me like a cloak. I really, really hoped that next time I called, Stuart would answer.

Chapter 34

STUART CLEANS IT UP

Each of us went to the police station in a different car, thoroughly patted down again and in handcuffs. There weren't enough available rooms to keep us separated in the station, so Millie was put into a holding cell, alone, and I was interrogated in the car. I answered every question to the best of my ability. I held up. I didn't cry.

A quick call to Stuart, who finally answered, got me out of the cuffs and given a cup of coffee. I was moved to a waiting area. The coffee tasted awful, even to my abused taste buds, and the clumpy powdered creamer didn't improve it much. But I had use of my hands. The handcuffs had been pretty inconvenient and even more embarrassing.

Joy – I didn't think of her as "the Floozy" anymore – and Fred the Philanderer were still being questioned, separately. Millie was singing. Quite literally. At least I thought it was her voice crooning

"Nobody knows the trouble I've seen" in a throaty and remarkably tuneful alto. She probably wasn't sober yet.

Stuart strode in. He looked like he had been orbiting Planet Nyquil and then crash-landed. But he still looked awfully good to me. He stopped in front of me and peered through rheumy eyes.

"You OK?"

I nodded.

"This wasn't supposed to be a tough assignment."

I nodded again.

"A short wait, a couple of photos, bingo," Stuart said.

I nodded very solemnly.

"Sorry, Hetta." Sincerity radiated from him.

I nodded yet again, but this time I burst into tears, too.

"Aw, Hetta…" Stuart took the coffee cup from my hand, spilling a little.

"Shit," he said, and set the cup on the plastic chair next to me. He shook a couple of drops of coffee off his hand, wiped it on his jeans, and then grasped my arms and lifted me to my feet. He drew me to his chest, where I bawled like a teenager who'd just found out the Boy of Her Dreams preferred her best friend. I snuffled and drooled and didn't care. Stuart just held onto me until I recovered enough to accept a wad of tissues from a hovering police officer. I had a crick in my neck from hiding my face in Stuart's chest, inconveniently located a couple of inches too low for comfortable crying.

Now I looked as wretched as Stuart.

"Can I go home?" I asked.

Stuart nodded. "But I'm going with you. Your place or mine?" He grinned as roguishly as someone fighting the Mother of All Colds could.

"Mine," I responded selfishly. "I have a guest room with a separate bath, and homemade chicken soup in the freezer, and you probably have a bag packed anyway."

"I do," said Stuart. "I expected as much." He grinned at me as I dabbed at my face and nose. "And I bet you have miso soup and tea, too, and plenty of tissues and juice."

I nodded. He told me to sit down again for a minute, then went with the police officer and spoke quietly for a few minutes while I found myself thirsty enough to finish the coffee. When Stuart returned, he smiled at me.

"We're good to go," he said. "You'll come back in the morning to answer some more questions, and I'll come with you. We'll get your car then. They're still sorting out the stories from the others, and trying to sober Millie up enough to get something coherent out of her. They said you gave a good, thorough statement," Stuart added. "Good job."

I snuffled again and let Stuart lead me outside to his medium blue four door sedan with no distinguishing features. I understood it now. It was a surveillance vehicle. Stuart was a perfect match for the car: no distinguishing features, hard to describe, medium everything and average everything. I thought about television and movie private investigators, and how hard it would be to keep a tall, hawk-featured and roughly handsome muscleman from being noticed.

And in the dark, quiet car ride to my home, I thought about how I went unnoticed. Women of mature years, with baggy jeans and comfortably soft and sagging bosoms, brown hair and less-than-striking profiles, blended into the scenery as surely as men like Stuart. I was scared and upset now, after looking down gun barrels and thinking on my feet, but while it had been happening, I'd been... alive.

Energized by adrenaline, I'd lived in the moment. I didn't need Stuart to tell me I'd done well, or the police officers; I knew I had. No one was dead, no one was injured, and all the criminals -- plus maybe an innocent or two -- had been apprehended and stories were being sorted by the police. I felt justice would be done, and

Millie would go on to live her life, and Joy and Fred would pay some sort of debt to society. And as I glanced at Stuart's unremarkable profile, alert to the traffic, I decided I wanted to do it again.

"Stuart?"

"Yeah?"

"Can I have another assignment or do I have to wait for you to be really sick again?"

He actually laughed. It sounded sort of like honking, but I could tell it was a laugh, because I've been around Stuart for a while.

"We'll talk in the morning."

"I did OK, didn't I?"

"You did great."

"Then get me a license."

"Good idea."

"Can I be Derek?"

"Sometimes," he agreed, as he pulled into my driveway. "We'll talk some more tomorrow, Spencer."

"As in Spencer the fictional private eye?"

"Except you're real."

"I am," I said as he parked the car in front of the garage and I released my seat belt. "Let's get some of that chicken soup and put you back in bed. My guest room is ready for you."

"Miso soup," said Stuart.

"With chicken broth?"

"Then it wouldn't be miso soup, would it?"

We smiled at each other and I burst out laughing when Stuart winked at me. I decided I'd bake Mitch a batch of my best walnut-oatmeal-chocolate chip cookies to thank him, again, for introducing me to the nonexistent Derek Irons.

Here is an excerpt from Hetta Moon's next adventure, *Full Moon Madness*, available in late 2019. For further updates, contact Carol at Carol.Yingling@gmail.com or through her website, www.CarolFreyYingling.com.

Chapter One

"Coffee?" I called to Stuart in his office. "I just made some."

"How bad is it?" Stuart responded, not unreasonably. My coffee making skills are infamous. Thirty-plus years of practice haven't improved them.

"Probably a 'two-extra-sugars' batch," I answered. Stuart drinks most coffee black and unsweetened. Mine, he takes recommendations.

"Please," came from the office. Stuart sounded distracted. Maybe this meant there's a new job to do. Since he found Mamie Robinson's Chihuahua on Tuesday, there had only been three phone calls. Two were from Stuart's mother in Homosassa, Florida, and the other was from Ray, who lines his hats with aluminum foil. Ray had called to report that he had found another bug in his bedroom, which was proof, once again, that he was being monitored by a) the CIA, b) aliens, c) members of the Soviet Russian government who are planning on staging a coup, or, and most probably, d) all of the above and possibly more. I'd told Ray to bring in the bug, which he did yesterday, and it still sat on my desk in a sandwich-size plastic bag. It was a small dead cockroach. Ray had been triumphant when he showed me, and pointed out how cleverly disguised the bugs were now. Stuart insisted I had to figure out how to file it. Stuart likes to give me crap sometimes. I am working out ways to press it, like a flower, and comply. Because I like to give Stuart crap back.

I repaired Stuart's coffee with two sugars and then brought it, with a coconut macaroon perched on a small brown napkin made of recycled paper, into his office. I bake good cookies. They sort of make up for my coffee.

Stuart, who is technically my boss but doesn't usually act like it, was hard at work hunched over his computer. Or so it seemed.

"Check THIS out!" he said, not taking his eyes off the screen. "Can you believe it?" He rolled back from his desk a few inches so I could see the screen more easily.

It was a photo of a stone. A gemstone of some kind, green and smooth, with a star-like design in the center.

"It's a honkin' big emerald. On Ebuy!" Stuart crowed.

I looked at the screen. "It doesn't look like an emerald. It looks like a star sapphire." I shrugged and moved a couple of papers on Stuart's desk to clear space for the mug. "Here's your coffee," I said, and placed the coffee and macaroon in front of him, carefully away from the computer mouse, which Stuart had been known to handle with great abandon when he's excited. And, for some reason, this semi-precious stone seemed exciting to Stuart.

"It's 92 carats and part of the Sandipur Empire's royal collection," explained Stuart, still looking at his computer screen instead of my macaroon.

Well, now I knew the reason for Stuart's excitement. That is indeed 'a honkin' big' gemstone. And the Sandipur Empire had been in the local news a lot lately, since the Crown Prince had chosen to attend an exclusive -- meaning "hideously expensive" -- private college nearby.

"Maybe they're selling it to pay for the prince's tuition," I said, and conjured up a little annoyance that my macaroon, a magnificent creation and much admired by fans of coconut, was receiving so little attention in the face of a stone which, albeit "honkin' big," was nevertheless merely a photo on a computer screen. While my macaroon was, so to speak, live and in person.

"And it's on Ebuy. How strange," said Stuart, who looked down at his coffee and spotted the cookie, too. "Is this one of your incredible macaroons?" he asked, and sniffed appreciatively, eyes closed.

"Yes. It's to make up for the quality of the coffee," I preened, all annoyance immediately forgotten. A macaroon in hand does beat a jewel on the screen, and all was right with the world again. At least I thought all was right in the world, sheltered as I was in the offices of Derek Irons, Private Investigator.

Titles by Carol Frey Yingling

writing as Carol L. Frey

NOTES FROM THE DOMESTIC
UNDERGROUND

NOTES FROM THE EQUESTRIAN
UNDERGROUND

SONGS OF LOVE